Life Line

Life Line

Michael Breslow

The Viking Press New York

First published in 1978 by The Viking Press
625 Madison Avenue, New York, N.Y. 10022

Published simultaneously in Canada by
Penguin Books Canada Limited

Printed in the United States of America

Set in Videocomp Century Expanded

ACKNOWLEDGMENT
New Directions Publishing Corp., JM Dent & Sons Ltd.,
and the Trustees for the Copyrights of the late Dylan Thomas:
Dylan Thomas, *Adventures in the Skin Trade*.
Copyright 1939 by New Directions Publishing Corp.
Reprinted by permission.

One chapter of this book originally appeared
in *Mississippi Review*, June 1973.

LIBRARY OF CONGRESS CATALOGING IN PUBLICATION DATA
Breslow, Michael.
    Life line.
    I. Title.
PZ4.B8426.Li   [PS3552.R392]   813'.5'4   77–9055
ISBN 0–670–27972–2

For Elizabeth

    my daughter
    upon whose back I wrote this book

And this is all there was
to it: a woman had been
born, not out of the womb,
but out of the soul and
the spinning head. And he
who had borne her out of
darkness loved his creation,
and she loved him. But this
is all there was to it: a
miracle befell a man. He
fell in love with it, but
could not keep it, and the
miracle passed. And with
him dwelt a dog, a mouse,
and a dark woman. The
woman went away, and the
dog died.

—DYLAN THOMAS,
"The Mouse and The Woman"

Life Line

Prologue

Two years ago, in 1975, a committee of scientists was formed to investigate the charge that I, Michael Halbgewachs, a researcher in cancer, wilfully falsified the results of an experiment, and turned against a public and a science that I was sworn to serve.

I had sought to prove that skin, when surgically removed from the body and stored in a refrigerator, loses its ability to provoke an immune response of rejection when transplanted to another, unrelated body. But it wasn't only the skin that concerned my jurors. It was the skin's connection to cancer that excited them, for they felt my work to be the key to the mystery of cancer's success. That if transplanted skin was able to escape the attention of its host, it would also show how cancer got away with it in the body of its victim. These two factors were related because it is now widely believed that cancer grows daily in the healthy body, and daily it is recognized and destroyed. The person who falls prey to cancer is one whose body is unable to recognize its strange presence and is thereby incapable of destroying it. With my deceit, they maintained, I had deserted the cancer patient and had immeasurably postponed his cure.

Brought before the committee that heard my case without me present was the accusation, made by a nurse's aide, that I had dyed a black patch on the head of a white subject to counterfeit successful skin transplants between two genetically incompatible human beings. The authenticity of all my work—my integrity as a man—was questioned. The committee's findings have never been made public, but following their secret "review," I was relieved of all my responsibilities. And what became known as the "Black Patch Episode" was buried along with me by my accusers. Before my final interment, a reviewer in the journal *Transplant* had this declaration to make:

If there is a sin in science, it must certainly be falsehood. For unlike the marketplace, progress in science is unable to stem from the lie. Scientific development needs trust at its very basis. An investigator who wilfully destroys that trust not only destroys himself in the act, but poisons the well from which others drink. Such a man must be driven out from the ranks, for just as he is today a contaminant, he poses a threat also into tomorrow.

Part One

i

For two years now I have been unable in any way to respond. Unable to know where or even how to begin. A vacuum slowly formed around me. I was shunned by my former colleagues and my so-called friends as though I had a terribly contagious disease. A disease that would prove fatal to all who contracted it. I became a leper. And in this state I have tried with all my might to forget my leprosy. I sought to remove all the mirrors, but unfailingly my hands would uncover the scabs and lumps. As insidious as the tumors I had dissected, the tentacles of what I am, who I have become, and what I did, spread deep into my mind. I found it difficult to get out of bed—to escape from unconsciousness—and would remain under my covers for hours after my body was geared to rise. My enemy in the morning was not my thoughts, but the cold wetness of spittle that my pillow pressed against my cheek. It succeeded in arousing me even though I was unwilling. I intended to remain inert, to ignore, to forget. It has been impossible.

In an effort to relieve what is for me unrelenting pressure, I have decided to attempt the telling of "my story." I do this filled with the fear not that the telling will fail to impress my judges or an audience that is unknown to me and naturally disinterested, but that it will not prevent the flood of forces which threaten to engulf me. My presentation will not be a scientific one —nor even directly concern science—I will not forward my arguments against those of my detractors so that the building blocks of discovery and the edifice of scientific truth may be built. Neither will I answer the "charges" as if I were the defendant in an action—I do not recognize the court. I will tell the story just so that it may be told and afford me some peace.

ii

To be a surgeon in a cancer hospital is to occupy a very special position. A position that changes your life. You are surrounded by the very sick and by the dying. There are no minor illnesses here. The only kind word is remission or reprieve. But for how long? No one really knows. For every part of the body, every cell, every organ, there is a cancer to devour it. The cancer wards are like the scenes of accidents. Catastrophic accidents that result in the loss of parts. Familiar parts like noses, jaws, breasts, cheeks, penises. Once the devastation has begun, there is almost no stopping the spread. Except by extraordinary means—like minor Hiroshimas, which halt the chaos but remove hair from the scalp in clumps with each rake of the comb. Or the chemotherapy, the chemicals that trick the cancer, that make it forget for a while who it is and where it's going. And the nausea and vomiting that follow the chemicals, especially in the very young. The names of these agents are beautiful, like Vincristine, and deadly, like Nitrogen Mustard, and sometimes forgetful where to stop, where the cancer ends, and continue until they have destroyed everything in their path. There is no way to avoid the sounds of all this, the screams, the moans, the shrieks. Even when locked behind doors, they pervade the buildings, dampen the silence, and demand recognition.

If the chemicals and the radiation fail, as often they do, then there is the knife. To cut the roots of the past and the path of the future, and to do it as if blindfolded. The surgery is radical, that is to say, more than what seems at the time to be enough. If there is a lump in the breast and it is malignant, then both the lump and the breast are removed. There is even a sculptor who makes extra faces for those who have lost one. And plumbers, who fashion human tubes and pipes. The combinations are endless and so is the misery. "Quality of life" is a phrase now in vogue with cancer specialists. Improving the quality of the patient's life if one is unable to prolong it. Have you ever seen a man who has lost the side of his face, who has a red rubber tube that hangs instead of a nose. Who is forced to travel in the subways. His quality of life is what they're talking about. And with the gadgets, with the tubes, there is the maintenance and the repairs. The lines in the clinic, each and every day, queued up for a pipe-straightening or a battery.

And when all fails, there is the morgue. But the waiting is not yet over. The clinic lines form again in the refrigerator room where the corpses wait for the last operation—the autopsy. Some of the bodies are hidden under sheets, others are covered with paper towels. Decomposition immediately replaces life and the room is filled with the odor of rot. A stink that clings to the skin and clothes of those who work in the morgue. A black body, distended in death, and covered by single sheets of white paper towels, like stones on a path leading from the abdomen to the chest, is a sight that I have seen in the morgue and cannot ever forget. It is the final disposition, the placing of the once animate human being squarely and irretrievably into the realm of death. There is no more reciprocity; the body returns no favors.

The actual job of the autopsy falls to the dieners, the morgue's laboratory attendants. The cutting room is large enough to accommodate six bodies which are autopsied by the dieners simultaneously. The bodies lie naked, except for an occasional wedding band, on metal trolleys called gurneys which are spaced unevenly throughout the room. The dieners work like any assembly line worker. The bodies are like balloons, flaccid without air. The mouths are open and sometimes the eyes. Penises, like silent cannons, rest pointing to the left and to the right, on motionless balls. Heads positioned too long in death become reservoirs of blood and turn the color of a beet. The room is unadorned except for a few chairs, tables along the walls, microscopes, and the instrument trays of the dieners.

First, the chest is opened by cutting through the sternum with a power saw. The smell of seared flesh fills the room. The dieners continue, they are immune. If the saw doesn't cut through the bone entirely, a chisel is hammered through the chest. The heart and lungs as well as the other viscera are removed for gross and microscopic examination. Later, the top of the head is sawed off, the diener grabbing the scalp with his one hand and the power saw with the other. The brain rarely escapes a slash of the saw, and is easily removed from its case. Once finished, the bodies are set aside, chests caved in and skulls uncapped. If there is an argument for the soul, it can be found in that room.

Under the microscope, the hidden cause of this devastation is uncovered. The mecademized layers of normal tissue, ordered cell by ordered cell, are invaded and disrupted by the cancer. A new architecture appears. An architecture of chaos. Haphazard and infiltrative growth in every plane, without purpose. The purple stain clearly outlines the process and the invisible cause of pain and suffering is brought to light. Becomes like an artwork, is appreciated morphologically and aesthetically, like a poisonous snake with beautiful markings safe behind glass.

iii

Escape to the outside becomes more frequent for me.
More necessary. My laboratory, the skin grafts, all become tedious. I write grant proposals, thoughtful, expeditious, critical: "The clinical and basic science implica-
tions of this proposal are such as to point up an obvious
and critical need for thoughtful, yet expeditious pursuit
of the principal investigator's observations . . ."

Visits to the hospital across the street become more
oppressive. My eyes photograph cameos of pain and
indelibly trace them onto my memory. A mother beside
her son, standing in a treatment room, fully clothed in
cloth coat with two full brown paper bags at her feet.
Bags filled with clothes. Clothes that never will be worn
by her son again. And the son, he is in the position of the
octopus. Tubes coming from every orifice of his body.
He is jumping with pain, a cancer acrobat. The image
does not leave me, the woman beside the bags, the boy.

It was at this time that I began to break away. I

11

remember returning to my laboratory. It was empty of people. The machinery stood idle. The cancer flees and no one is in pursuit. I had, I thought then, momentarily lost my willingness. The willingness of the hunter to persevere. To steadfastly stalk and finally kill. It was not to pass in a moment, though. It was to continue until I could barely step into the laboratory. All of my discipline, my energy, escaped.

That day I repeated an act of my youth. I visited a whorehouse. I include it here on purpose. I include it because it marked the beginning of a change in my life. A change and, later, a connection that forms the very basis of this statement.

Warmth radiating from my groin in waves. A depolarization. Displacing the cancer dread, the life dread. The receptionist of the whorehouse, the "madam," describing over the telephone the location, the wares, the flesh. Seemingly perfect breasts, hips, asses, mouths, all without blemish, without disease. I walk swiftly to my car, imbued with purpose. I am excited; there is the danger of violence, of the police, of publicity, of losing my position as healer and mind photographer, of sinking low with syphilis, and of disappearing. I go anyway. I cross the bridge and enter the southbound stream of the East River Drive. Every kind of car, every kind of face, of person, of interest, of meaning behind the wheel, all involved in the race. The cars cutting in front of one another, behind, and around, all wanting to be first. To arrive. To win. A chorus of Greek-owned coffee shops along the road applauding with hamburgers, cole slaw, news of Popadopoulos. New York a heart pounding in arrhythmia. Fibrillating. And me speeding down its aorta to a whorehouse.

A brownstone in the Thirties. And behind its polite facade, the whorehouse. Enter Dr. Livingstone. The whores seated watching the soap opera on TV. Their shoes are cadillacs for the feet, and their legs, encased in black nylon stockings, are runways. I take this all in slowly, and more. The breasts. The lips. The eyes. The hair. Disarticulated at first, then the composite. The whores stand, they curtsy, they pirouette. I'm introduced to one, then to another. "Who would you like?" I'm asked. "I'm not sure," I reply. The receptionist is back on the phone. "For forty dollars you can have any girl, for as many times as you like, and for anything you like. Except Greek. Only Mary will go Greek, but for ten dollars extra."

I make my choice. She is Latin, large breasted, and she smiles in agreement. I'm led into a bedroom. The blinds are drawn and the only furniture is a bed and a nightstand. It reminds me of a treatment room, with its tissue dispenser and ointments standing at the ready. She leaves, telling me that after I undress she will return. I undress quickly, in both fear and anticipation. My mind menu obscures every other thought. She is back. She asks for the money and puts it into the pocket of her robe. She kisses me and takes her robe off; it falls to the floor. She is naked except for her shoes. Her name is

Anna, she says, and sinks to her knees. She brings my cock to her mouth and begins to suck. "Do you want to fuck me?" she asks.

I dress and return to being the doctor. The scientist. Now satiated. Not by the conquest of cancer but by having lain with a whore. Touched, felt, excited the whore who besides her calling is also a woman, a human being, who claims to be called Anna, and who, if not really moved by my caress, has culpable and palpable erectile tissue which has enlarged at my touch. Inoculated now, filled with artifice but also with warmth that is for me, at first, real, I head back to the island, to my laboratory and the hospital.

iv

Days later. Five o'clock in the morning. I have a long-awaited appointment with the Director of the Institute. The Director begins his workday early—there is much for him to do if he is going to slay Cancer and win the Prize. His office and apartments are in a penthouse on top of the hospital, twenty stories above the island's only street. From the windows of the waiting room one can see a large part of Manhattan, an awesome sight that entices one to believe he is on top of the world.

The waiting room is decorated with portraits of other great men of science, past directors of the Institute, who, in tailored suits framed by gold, look down gravely at those seated below, waiting to see their successor. For eighteen floors beneath the Director's office are hospital rooms occupied by the cancer patients. The Director rides this undulating wave and by carefully leading his army of scientists, seeks relentlessly to break the back of cancer.

15

His door opens and out steps a party of Korean doctors; they are bowing profusely, their mouths displaying billboards of teeth. They are working on the development of an immunotherapy for leprosy. They continue out the 'door, backwards, with all due respect for the Director, who follows. He is an impressive man. A giant of sorts. He is wearing a sports shirt and western boots. These are his trademark. Only on grand rounds does he wear a lab coat. He warmly invites me in.

His recent appearance in a popular magazine has brought him into the households of America. He is portrayed as a self-made man. One who overcame the odds and then surpassed the doubters. Injured early in his career by a car accident that left him crippled, he swore that he would walk again. And he made good that promise. The son of a farmer, he has that Midwestern affability and charm that often hides the machinery of power and aggression that shallowly lies beneath. He has the physical girth of a hero, with the type of rough-hewn face that is said to show character. And, there is also the warmth he possesses—that easily flows when he treats children. On rounds he actively touches his young patients, he does not shrink from them and their disease as many others do. I have often believed that, if he could, he would relieve their fatal burdens by assuming them himself. But I have never mistaken the appetite of the man. It is the appetite of America, the drilling, the pumping, the neon, the insatiable drive for power and conquest.

This was the last time I was to meet with him privately. I remember him standing by the window next to his table-high globe of the world. Through the window, he is framed by the mammoth girders of the Triborough Bridge.

"Michael," he begins. "I'm glad to see you this morning. I'm sorry there hasn't been time before." He sits down at the edge of his monumental desk. I snatch a look at the triptych photographs of his family. He sees my escape and becomes stern, impatient. "Listen, there are problems with your work. Problems of repeatability. Of the three labs that are working on confirming your results—Weinberger's, Krone's, and Malmquist's—not one has had any success. I know that you believe they're using improper technique. But, nonetheless, they're all reporting failure. There is some talk . . ."

I open my mouth to speak, not quite sure that the words of defense will flow. Not sure as to why I'm about to defend myself. I study the Director's face, look into his uncompromising eyes—feel the energy that took him out of the wheelchair. He becomes for a moment my father, my father framed by diplomas, by endorsements from all over the world, pictures of the powerful with autographs scrawled across them, surgeons in the operating room, and old professors standing beside their accomplished pupil. I want to tell the transmogrified Director the real problems of my research. Not how work in California on refrigerated human blood lymphocytes has had results similar to my own, but, instead, how I can no longer spend time in the laboratory, how I cannot bear watching the cancer, the crazy cells, the

17

mutilated bodies, feeling the death that hangs over the place. Meekly, I discuss the lymphocytes.

He walks over to me and places his right hand on my shoulder. I feel the connection enter like a pulse into my body. He is transfusing his energy into me. "I have no doubt that the results you published are true. I have complete faith in you. You have realized in your work what I view as the keystone of our entire program—if we can understand the molecular basis of the failure to reject, then there will be nothing stopping us. We will be able to engineer the cell, recover tissue and organs that were lost to disease. The whole field of transplantation will be revolutionized with universal donors and organ banks made possible. And, of course, cancer. We will know the mechanism, have it by the throat." His eyes gleam and he shakes me violently with his hand. "Volner," he says slowly, almost as if it were an oversight, his eyes and face returning to their normal elasticity, "is attempting to duplicate your findings in Cambridge. In six months he will report his findings to the Institute. They must confirm yours."

I nod. The way a ventriloquist's dummy nods. My head moving back and forth in circumscribed acknowledgment. He sits down behind his desk and lifts up a bottle of Ambassador Scotch to show me. "Ravi gave me this." He is demonstrating loyalty. Ravi and his microbiologist wife are well liked by the Director. They are producing and they are loyal. I am standing before him ready to go, to escape, but he has me firmly grasped in his power. With his long, manicured nails he begins to meticulously pick at the Ambassador's ribboned medallion that ornaments the bottle until he has pulled it entirely away from the rest of the label. "How does it look?" he says, placing the medal against his chest.

V

I remember returning to my laboratory and for a few hours was fervent to reorder my work so as to prove definitively my earlier findings. But, like an anesthetic, the effect of the Director's words soon began to wear off. And in their place came the emptiness that is now never far away. Like a low gentle tide it came, until I was enveloped. All energy for work dissipated. I sat at my desk and stared straight ahead. I answered the questions of my associates by rote and I am surprised that they never realized my condition. Finally, I couldn't remain seated any longer. I decided to visit the setting of my experiment, the laminar-flow room, a special germ-free environment that housed my two subjects.

On a special wing of the Institute is a ward devoted to experiments with human subjects. For many of these subjects it is a court of last resort, where conventional therapies have failed and a reasonable hope of cure has passed, leaving room only for miracles. The status of patient here is reduced to that of experimental subject, to human guinea pig, and improvement is equivalent to a breakthrough in science.

In a corner of this ward a laminar-flow room was constructed. It contained two beds divided by a glass partition and was totally surrounded by a waterfall flow of air, from the ceiling to the floor, whose wall-like currents keep bacterial infiltration to a minimum. Originally designed for organ-transplant patients, where immunological resistance is purposely reduced so as to enable the "take" of foreign tissue, it was now the home of my two subjects, whose skin would be transplanted without such immunosuppression.

The donor in this case was black, the recipient white. Genetically incompatible, they would provide irrefutable proof of my transplantation technique. Putting a gown over my street clothes, I approached the black subject's bed. We exchanged no greetings, for although he was alive, he was no longer of this world. In place in his mouth was a heavy rubber endotracheal tube, an air pipe that was secured by several turns of adhesive tape wound around his head. His eyes were open, bloodshot, focusing on nothing. He was a gift of the state, a prison inmate who had been stabbed fifteen times in the chest with an ice-pick but refused to die. He lay in a decorticate posture, his only organic utterances were the heart and brain waves emitted by what was left of his nervous system. He was now primeval, his brain reduced to that of a reptile, the precursor of what he once enjoyed. Spike after spike danced his heart and brain on the monitor over his bed, a steady cadence that promised not to cease until I had stripped him further of some skin to be transplanted to his white neighbor. I lifted up his covers to inspect the Foley catheter that entered his penis and carried away his involuntary output of urine to a series of bottles underneath the bed.

I painted his penis with Betadine solution to prevent infection; the brush strokes no longer provoked any reaction. I inspected his head, the purple lips swollen and cracked, the teeth yellow and loosely set surrounding the tube. Out of his mouth came the odor of decay caused by the bacteria that had moved in with the tube and taken up permanent residence beneath his tongue. The smell was so profound that I began to retch, and had difficulty in aiming an eyedropperful of methyl cellulose into his unblinking eyes, to prevent their drying out. The missed shots ran down his forehead and cheeks. I entered my maintenance orders into his chart and went to visit his neighbor on the other side of the glass.

"How are you, Doc? I see you was saying hello to my friend next door, and I was getting kinda jealous of the attention you was giving him."

"I'm fine, Mr. Lukash, and the nurse tells me you're doing real well. I stopped in to tell you that we're almost ready with the experimental protocol, the design. When all the wrinkles are ironed out, we'll take some skin from your friend next door and transplant it on to you. Are you still willing to give it a go?"

"You know I am, Doc. Like Dr. Jacobsen says, if I gotta be here, I might as well help you guys out. The only thing was my wife, you know, she was concerned cause the guy was colored. But I told her that where I was going, a little patchwork wouldn't matter. I watch him sometimes, when they forget to pull the curtain, like sometimes when they're changing him, and, you know, he gives me the willies. But I don't mind. If I can help you I'll feel good. It's just the laying here that drives me crazy. Christ, if there was no TV, I'd really go bananas, as it is. . . . You know, Doc, will I ever get out of here?"

I looked at Lukash beneath me, his whole countenance eager to please—as if he could cajole me into curing him, his taking the Negro's skin as the first down payment. He knew the probable outcome of his disease —a coal miner for thirty years whose lungs were pin cushions embedded with glass—its slow, lethal progress with little organ involvement, and he knew I knew. But he watched for any little slip, any gesture that would belie what I'd already said. I explained to him again the purpose of our experiment, how it would benefit mankind, children, small dumb animals; how it would give him something purposeful to do with his life; how it would make us famous, and help entertain that poor nigger next door. I pointed out the signature blanks on the consent form, and with a childlike scrawl, Anthony Lukash became a volunteer. The nursing shift was changing, and the charge nurse appeared at the door beaming. "How are *we* doing today, Mr. Lukash?" I ordered Demerol for Lukash, to help him sleep, and changing places with the nurse, escaped his embrace.

23

vi

In this beginning I wonder about the purpose of these words—this statement, as I put it—this parade. A parade that takes the reader also into whorehouses. What is the worth of all this? Will it guarantee me restitution? Integrity? And though I can hardly continue, I cannot stop either. Each halt, every dry spell, grabs hold and twists my insides.

There is a cripple who lives in an apartment across the street. His window faces mine, and every time I look out he is there facing me—like the reflection in a mirror. He is a very fastidious cripple. He appears always to have just had a haircut. And bordering his shiny jet black hair —he is Chinese—are wide avenues surrounding the ears and a boulevard of a part that adds to the stability of his life. He is maintained to my eyes across the street by a haircut, and by neatly pressed pants that flap around his atrophied legs (he comes outside occasionally to dust his car with a whisk broom). But, of course, his stability—

his persisting appearance—rests on much more. On resignation. The resignation of a cripple—one who knows
that his legs will not afford running. I therefore ask
your patience in the reading of this statement if the gait
is faulty—if just out of the morgue you are brought into
the whorehouse. It is only because I have not yet
learned my lesson.

Soon after seeing the Director, I proposed a protocol
of activity for my laboratory associates. My goal was to
extend my observations about the transplantability of
refrigerated animal skin to humans and to other organs.
I intended to prove that the refrigeration of excised skin
did indeed alter antigenicity—as I had observed—and,
in addition, sought to explain why. By using our two
subjects, the one white, the other black, I would show
once and for all that skin stored in a refrigerator for five
to seven days could be transplanted to genetically incompatible human beings without being rejected. My
associates were enthused by the challenge, and I was
their cheerleader, but my spirit was no longer involved.
I spent less time in the laboratory and more in the clinic.
And the more I was involved in the never-ending mass
of illness and despair, the less I could tolerate the enter-
prise at all. Of course it should have been otherwise. My
training and motivation should have mediated my feelings. I had always wanted the power to heal. I had been
educated to heal. And I had always taken great satisfac-
tion in the ability to reduce suffering. But the cancer had
jumped its boundaries. It no longer was contained by the
patients and their agonized relatives. My primitive an-

swers and drawing-board therapies were not enough to stem the tide. The cancer leaped across the divide and invaded me. There was no longer any separation. No longer any clinical dispassion. Visits to the terminally ill —where devastated bodies were supported by respirators in order to oxygenate a life that no longer could breathe, to shock a heart filled to burst with tumor into activity—were more than I could bear. And the eyes that met mine—the eyes that contained the supreme truth, that could see the future, knew the chart, could read the hieroglyphs of the electrocardiogram and the electroencephalogram monitors, crack the code on the immutable porcelain of nurses' faces, and challenge my own with their terrible knowledge—those eyes I could no longer face.

The color plates of medical texts which illustrate disease in its convoluted forms are easily remembered by the student. In the same format I can see a plate of myself, full front and nude, entitled "Forced to resort to prostitutes." A history would follow in the text with a discussion at the end. The physics of choice would be explored, the alternatives neatly parsed, the aberration diagnosed, and illness decreed. The process was not that easy for me, however. For one thing, I was not forced. But neither did I run. Is it too romantic, this retrospective notion that I was a soldier in a war zone? No one will argue that it wasn't a war I was engaged in, that the victims that constantly surrounded me were there as a result of terrorism. I can only say that I began to visit whorehouses in my escape from death. And when I found life masquerading as death in one of them, it was against the laws of probability, for the whorehouse, I had discovered, is not unlike the refrigerator room of the morgue where bodies become balloons.

These whorehouse escapes would inevitably lead me to death once more. For all the pretended passion, and even the real, when it so rarely and involuntarily escaped, there was the brutality and self-degradation of the act. The demanded servility of the whore. The taking of pleasure by force of money without the least desire to repay. Indeed, the taking of that pleasure by causing pain. And while in the throes of this passion play—while the whore is on her knees, her shoes biting into her feet, she opens the valves in her throat, or with her head buried deep in a pillow at a forty-five-degree angle to her ass, she relaxes her sphincter—to believe that it is pleasure instead of riding a crazy bronco to death, that is the coldest irony of all.

vii

But knowledge wasn't enough to stop me. I rode the clothesline from the one death house to the other.

40–22–36

HI, I'M KIM!

(the ad read)

This is my first advertisement, and I admit, I am more than a little nervous. I am a former stewardess, 21 years old, who has decided to go professional. I have been told that I am very attractive, and while I was flying, hardly a trip would pass without my being propositioned. So why not, I thought. I am tall, my breasts full and firm, and my disposition easy. My favorite way to get to know you is by exploring with my tongue every nook and cranny of your body. And once you're ready, and I mean ready to remove anything that stands in your way, my body is all yours. I will be at the mercy of all your fantasies. I will do whatever you command, what you've always wanted from a woman but were afraid to ask. And once you've come, once I've sucked you dry, I am yours again.

If you would like to meet me today, call me to visit in my very
private Eastside apartment. 10–12.

(212) 555–9641

And, once again, I fled downtown to the source of this
never-placed-before advertisement. I remember the ve-
locity of those southbound trips on the FDR quite viv-
idly. The car was propelled by my body, not only in
response to the ad, or how I had embellished it or what
I edited out of it, but in response to what I sought to
force altogether from my mind—my pathetic attempt at
human contact, which quickly usurped the mechanics of
fluid and the swell of fantasy and replaced it with terrible loneliness.

The speed at which I flew was also related to my being
a native son. Born in Brooklyn, I could never lay claim
to Manhattan as being my own—of my making—it was
not even an inheritance, though pockets like the Lower
East Side once sheltered my parents, and the high
schools of the city had educated them. The island of
Manhattan was ruled by outsiders, by people from Ne-
braska—with fair hair and blue eyes, they were the
directors—the puppetmasters who perpetuated the
myth that the real capital of New York City was the
garment district, not Wall Street or the American Yacht
Club. I sped over this city, for I thought myself no more
a part of it than the factory workers who had replaced
my relatives. I was simply a pieceworker cutting a more
involved design.

And the pieceworker was greeted at the whorehouse

door and ushered inside. The madam of this house was no veteran whore; small, studious-looking, brown hair pulled back in a tight bun, she could have been a student of English literature, and, in fact, once was. That is until her boyfriend, with the help of those who insure such businesses, opened his own house. The girls who weren't busy sat in the sitting room of this three-bedroom apartment, and smiled demurely as they shifted their working anatomy into sharper focus. Their breasts vied for attention and their long legs opened and closed while the fantasies of the judges seated across the room enlivened the possibilities of each. There is more polarization in a whorehouse than at a college mixer, even though the outcome is fixed in advance.

The whores are not yet whores in the sitting room, they are only the promise of whores—the potentiality—and the johns, they appear to be disinterested, no longer ravenous, just curious, as they leaf through magazines and absentmindedly glance across the room. But the pretense is quickly dropped when a just-finished girl returns into view, for now a choice must be made, the right delivery system picked if there is to be a payload. Nets could now be woven from the acknowledged lines of contact in the room, and if the TV or the cheap furnishings exert a coercive influence, they are quickly lost to the drama at hand.

It was my turn to choose. And I chose to go with "Vicki," who had been occupied in one of the bedrooms and hidden from my view. She was in her late twenties,

I would say, and had no difficulty with her role. This was important to me of course. I didn't want to find out as I lay naked and flat on my back that Vicki disliked being a whore. The only motivation the john really wants to hear about is a sexual one. He will settle for reasons of poor alternatives. "Working in an office is like being a whore." Or "My husband left us and I needed to get some money together for my kids." Or "My mother needed this operation." But what he really wants is, "I like to fuck, plain and simple, and where else could I get paid to do it?" "The only really good thing I do is sucking cock, and I like to do what I can do best." With Vicki it wasn't necessary to ask. Her ass led the way into the bedroom, and her black nylon stockings suspended from a garter belt and ending in platform shoes gave their own testament. Vicki was an Italian of exceptionally good looks who was blond. Not naturally blond, but pastel.

Before asking me my preferences, she told me to undress and then said she would return. It was a matter of the law, to protect against entrapment by a vice squad policeman posing as a john. She left the room, closing the door behind her. It was at this time I felt most vulnerable. Isolated in the room, removing my clothes, I was naked before she stripped away what little covered her body, I was naked before the act. I was no longer the visiting scholar but would be subject to the same close scrutiny applied to herself and her comrades outside in the sitting room. I would become—without my shirt, tie, and pants—her equal; and in this zone of suspended animation became as fragile and submissive as I would later demand her to be.

I folded my clothes neatly on an armchair that faced the bed. At least they would be unruffled. The room lay in the back of this floor-through brownstone apartment and had been reduced by subdivision to half its original size. But traces of its old elegance still remained, the mahogany woodwork beside the modernly sterile off-white walls whose only decoration was a mirror. Venetian blinds were closed over the one large window that faced the courtyard in back of the house and hid from the view of this proud old neighborhood the commerce and activity inside. It amused me that perhaps next door lived the hospital-trustee wife of some chemicals executive, who, watching Julia Child in her custom kitchen, was ignorant of the whorehouse next door and of the blowjobs that were taking place on the other side of her wall as she assiduously prepared with Julia a *pot de crème* to surprise her husband.

I was standing naked at the window when Vicki returned. She asked me to give her the money and lie down. She knelt down to inspect the health of my cock, apologizing for her clinical attitude, and then she bent over and kissed the tip, telling me she would be right back. In a moment she was, and while I watched with my arms folded behind my head, she began to strip and take me on the journey.

Slowly, enticingly, she removed her short smock, smiling knowingly, her eyes fixed on mine. Then she brought her hands back and freed her breasts, which sprang forward, the nipples erect. She was naked now except for her suspenders, stockings, and shoes, which she asked me if I minded her keeping on. I smiled. She sat down on the bed and I placed my hand in hers. I began to escape over her body, caressing her breasts, her face, her waist and thighs. She took me inside her mouth and slowly drew me out. For minutes I was lost in her body, and then it was over. The excitement was quickly replaced by the surrounding reality. We had a postprandial smoke and traded banalities but could no longer maintain the charade. So that when there was a knock on the door and the voice called out "Vicki," signalling that our time was up, there was no difficulty for me in leaving her bed.

Part Two

i

What's your complaint? you're yelling. Who d'ya think you are? What's all this about whores, cancer hospitals, science? We've heard all this before. Give us blood! Tissue! That's what we want! Show us you're innocent!

The telling is like an operation. The anesthetic hasn't been given yet. The patient is still awake. The scrub nurses are falling over each other laughing at the size of the guy's balls. Calling their cronies from the other operating rooms to come have a look. A tube is stuck into the throat. One in the cock. And a thermometer cable is fed up the ass. The show is on. The surgeon ready, rollicking with laughter at something his partner just said, accidentally disengaging the towel clips and drapes that are clamped through the skin. The skin pierced. Then cut open. At the Langer lines, so it will fit back together again. Like a custom-made suit. The first assistant sneezes. Which is only natural. Like the blood vessel that is ripped apart by the movement, and the blood that hits the lamps overhead. The anesthetist, where's he? He's outside, catching a smoke. But this isn't a surgery class, you say. What's the point? How does it add up? And you're right. Why don't I get on with the strip? And I will, but right now I'm busy clawing, at my head, my scalp scabs, starting to pull, rip into myself at the very roots, past the squamous epithelium, hoping to get past the skull and rub my hands in my brains, wash them there, in the grey matter and the blood, fill my fingernails with the muck, the clots, the nerves.

ii

Karin. Never had I met a more beautiful woman. "Don't worry about me," she said at the start. "I'm a little crazy. Do you know," she continued in her germanized English, "that a professor comes up here to visit me. He's a retired brain surgeon. And he's eighty-five years old." She giggles. And when she giggles, her eyes— which are light blue—twinkle. She is Peter Pan. Peter Pan in the whorehouse. "He doesn't want to screw, just to sit, you know, and talk. I love him. Sometimes he just sits for fifteen minutes recovering from climbing the stairs. He pays me to talk, can you believe it?" She is a woman-child, with *Spinnenbeinen,* spider's legs, long and lanky. Blond hair in a boy's haircut. Von Stauffenberg, I tell her, is my name and flash my most Germanic look at her—dilating my own blue eyes like four-inch naval guns. I am attempting seduction. In a whorehouse.

She is the daughter of a high-ranking officer—a

politico—an SS adjutant to Rommel in North Afrika. "He was so important," she laughs, "that when he was captured they kept him in Arizona. He hates America now, all cowboys he thinks. Today, he's an industrialist. Heavy machinery." Back to her body, my hands, my mouth. I am like a galvanometer. It isn't just the sex— we mix, this German and Jew—it's something else, something inside that I know, have felt before, but can't name.

"Do you know," she says afterwards, smiling brightly, "you're a good lay." I see the neurosurgeon in my mind, climbing the stairs behind me, his heart in tachycardia, beating like a taxi meter, he is next, his story is next to be told. The story of his life. Not mine, I think, as I try to draw her out. But she is closed. Like a clam. Like the blinds that shut out the sun from the room. "Why have you come here?" she asks. So innocently that I tell her.

"I'm a doctor. I work in a cancer hospital. You know, the Institute on Little Brother Island. In the East River." I smile—or did I not smile—was I serious—was I televising? "I come here to escape from the death."

"Do you know," she says, "I too have something to do with that Institute. It is very ironic." The "Do you know?" of the child. The woman-child. "You must go now," she says in response to the loud knock on the door. "Please come back. I would like to see you again." I kiss her on the cheek.

iii

Later that afternoon, our donor was scheduled for graft removal. A preliminary survey of his left thigh showed a possible yield of two hundred square inches of skin by complete decortication. It was much more than enough. I said hello to Lukash, told him what we were about to do with his neighbor, and went next door into the donor's room. He lay on his bed like a fish finally subdued at the bottom of the boat, the capturing line still connected to his mouth. The excursions of his chest were regular and his femoral pulse taken at the groin was strong and rhythmic. I began by shaving his thigh with a safety razor, getting the feel of the terrain. Next, I bathed the thigh with soap, water, and ether. The grafting would be easy as his thigh was large and muscular. In his walking and running days it must have served him well. Now it would serve science. After thoroughly cleaning the area, I painted it with one-percent tincture of iodine and, putting on gloves, hung the drapes. Blue, sterile towels were clipped with puncturing clamps to the skin, demarcating the surgical zone, and producing trickles of blood at each point of connection.

The donor remained unmoved at this assault. His nervous system no longer reached that far. I went to the sink to scrub, first cleaning my nails with the pick and then scrubbing my hands until they were raw. Sterile Vaseline was now rubbed on the donor's thigh to remove any friction from the path of the knife. I pulled up a roll of the greased black thigh with my gloved hand, and explained to the resident assisting me the direction I would take and the thickness that was required. A Ferris-Smith knife, with a ribbed back and razor-steel blade eighteen centimeters long, was pressed into my hand. Two vacuum-cleaner-like suction retractors were spread by the assistant in opposite directions on the thigh, creating a flat cutting surface. I took one of the retractors with my left hand, moving it about one inch in advance of the knife on the lubricated flesh, the assistant making counter traction with the other retractor. One long, steady cut freed a twelve-by-four piece of skin that would be adequate for our grafting purposes. There was only one bleeder, which was successfully tied off with 3-0 waxed white silk. The wound was dressed and the graft put on a flat metal specimen tray and sent downstairs to the laboratory refrigerator. Seven days later it would be sewn on to Lukash's forehead, and be visible proof of what the body would accept with a little mediation on our part. The donor was none the worse for the procedure and stared as patiently as ever at the ceiling. Into his unblinking eyes I dropped the methyl cellulose solution that would prevent them from drying out and rotting.

iv

The next time I see Karin, I gently explore the mystery of how she is connected to the Institute. "I was there," she says without emotion, "for some tests." She hesitates, but continues, after all we are both on a bed naked, but, yet, this is a whorehouse, and the basic premise of the whorehouse is the lie. Suddenly she flicks her wrist in front of my face. There is a raised scar that follows a zig-zag pattern across the surface. Its lines suggest no therapeutic purpose. "They told me I had this form of leukemia—blood cancer, you know, but that it was very rare. They had never had a case like it before. A doctor who was there, Rosenbaum, or Rosenberg, I think, you know, some German-Jewish name (she smiles), told me that when I died they would name the disease after me. So I went home from the hospital that day—Brian, my husband, wasn't home yet from work, and Molly was still at Brian's sister's house. I locked the door and closed the blinds and walked into the bathroom, where Brian kept his razor. I remember so clearly how much I wanted to die. How afraid I was of living out the year they gave me. They said, you will probably die within a year, there is nothing we can do. I was afraid. Afraid of waiting. I couldn't bear leaving my daughter. Not seeing her again. So I sat down on the side of the tub and opened my veins with the razor. How white that bathroom was to me that day. The tub. The tiles on the floor. And how unafraid of killing myself I was. I watched the blood—the dark red blood—fill each of the tiles at my feet. Fill one, then the next. But, they found me, forced the door somehow, took me to the hospital. Brian's sister came with Molly and found me. I'm sorry for telling you all this. You didn't come to hear my problems."

"Listen motherfucker," came like a bullet through the wall of our room, "I ain't getting ripped-off. She said I hadta wear a rubber and I ain't payin' forty dollars to wear no rubber. And I ain't payin' it to get jerked off. I can do that myself." "Come into the kitchen, please," a man's voice calmly answered.

"Please," I told Karin, "I never want to see you here again. Anywhere outside, just not here."

"Next week," she said, almost without emotion, "how about some place in the city. The museum, the Metropolitan. Is that okay? Thursday, at noon."

We dressed, hardly looking at each other. Afraid. She told me to wait for her downstairs. In a few minutes she appeared. In her street clothes, black and smartly tailored, she took on the part of suburban housewife, the

45

grown-up, and as the black garage attendant opened the door of her car, she entered without looking at him, pressed a folded bill into his hand, and sped away. With Connecticut plates. A long way off from a midtown whorehouse.

V

It wasn't only visiting privileges that I wanted from Karin. I wanted her for myself, and not for any other man, not even the aged neurosurgeon who came to share with her the telling of his life. My fingertips met no resistance on her body. I wanted her for the life she still possessed. The life she struggled to maintain as she ran. I wanted that life breathed into me; though of course I hadn't realized it then. I wanted it to mingle in my mouth, join my own breath. It was not only her beauty, nor the fact she was German, which certainly played a part; it was her *spirit* I loved even more than her face, for it came from desperation, desperation that matched my own.

I spent the week wondering whether Karin would charge me for seeing her; although we hadn't discussed it, I was sure she wouldn't. But what if she did? What would my reaction be? I drowned the thought out of my mind. I anticipated the meeting with all my energy.

I checked the Hematology clinic for her file. It wasn't listed under Karin anyone, the name she had given me. I asked the clinic secretaries, they knew nobody matching her description. I wondered whether I had been deceived. The recipient of a last trick.

But when Thursday came, there she was, climbing the great steps of the museum, smiling, nervous, and ready to go. Forgetting art, we got into my car and sped to Greenwich Village, an area her husband had warned her to steer clear of. The queers, he said, and the hippies—all filth. The soul food restaurant on Bleecker near Barrow was none of that. We brought in a bottle of wine, discreetly keeping it wrapped on the table, and ate chitlins and black-eyed peas for the first time in our white lives. And what was good about the Village filtered through the pink-curtained windows of the restaurant, leaving the rest outside; while, for us, a settlement of sorts was taking place, a negotiation between death runners and the unknown—a truce with time. What the physicists call a localized reversal of entropy, like an umbrella that shields you from the shit that flies every which way.

A lot she told me that afternoon. About her brother Johann, a psychiatrist in Germany. And about his friend the Baron who drove his Maserati through the streets of Heidelberg like a maniac, like you, she said, and about how much she was enjoying the forbidden city of New York. It was for us then an exciting adventure, one without a moral. We walked down Bleecker Street toward Christopher, past the antique shops and groceries.

We were at peace with the city, with each other—and the death, the leukemia, was left for a while behind.

While an undergraduate at City College, I used to ride the IRT—what we called the "San Juan Local"—up from Brooklyn to the campus stop at 137th Street. One night, going back home, I sat alongside some classmates opposite a sleeping black man who had nodded-out on wine. His face was marked with scars and scabs and his clothes were filthy and decayed. With each turn and jerk of the subway train, his torso, as if on a hinge, would swing back and forth, and his empty wine flask would sail up and down the corn-kerneled seats until it reached the invisible line of demarcation—the territory occupied by a sober Irish workingman, complete with lunch pail, who eyed the tide-swept bottle and its former owner with so much contempt that this energy alone could have shattered the flask. Regardless, back and forth the bottle went. A patrolling Transit Authority patrolman came into the car and the offended Irishman pointed a finger at the bottle and its owner. With a certain unconscious flair, the bum had crossed his legs, exposing the punctured sole of his shoe to the advancing policeman. SWAT, with a vengance, the cop brought his club against the sleeping man's shoe and he sprung wide awake. "Sleep here," said the cop, "and you're gonna pull some time." "Time," answered the black, without batting an eyelash, aiming a smile directly at us, "time is a unit of space."

Within that space ran Karin and me—and without, on the one side, her husband and child; on the other, leukemia, with the Institute's timetable. Our afternoons in the future would always end at four, enabling her to change lives, to negotiate the highways that spanned her two different worlds.

Above us in the beginning, so softly that only the convection of air could be felt, was the *moloch hamuvos*, the angel of death, who shared our bed. My colleagues know this angel well in the case of leukemia, the one with the foreshortened twenty-first chromosome, the one they call the Philadelphia chromosome in honor of the birthplace of its name. And at times, other afternoons, now spent in my Brooklyn apartment, the Philadelphia angel would come into bed with us, slip under the covers and lay his cadaverous hands between our bodies, cause them to shrink, prematurely separate us, and instill, in his inimitable way, a terrible fear. For we, in our own way, had found a wonderful peace, a peace that we wanted to last forever. Like Jews in an attic we hid, this SS-man's daughter and me, we hid from the angel who was also driven with a manifest destiny, the lengthening of his foreshortened twenty-first arm. But the sun, unbiased, would filter into the bedroom, illuminating the black and white print of Burne-Jones's "The Angels of Creation," which hung on the wall opposite our bed. And with the resiliency of brain tissue—the tissue so delicate that when starved it is the first in the body to die—we thought that these good spirits would protect us and push their handicapped brother from our minds.

I grew up in this Brooklyn I now shared with Karin. Lived for some twenty years in a three-room apartment not too far away from where we now met. I knew the streets and the parks intimately, for it was on the streets and in the parks that I escaped the madness of my family's life.

vi

One day I took Karin across Prospect Park to revisit the apartment house that was once my home. We walked past Kingston Avenue, where a mansion formerly owned by New York's most famous abortionist was now the headquarters of the *Lubovitcher Rebe,* a world-famous mystic, whose *Hasidic* followers in their black coats, earlocks and beards, lived in the nucleus of their own world. It was Jews such as these, I remarked to Karin, that the Nazis thought particularly reprehensible. They stuck out, were obviously different and clannish like the gypsies.

Some ten blocks later we reached the neighborhood of my youth. The apartment house was still there, its ninety families now black, its baroque lobby dark and empty, the furniture gone along with the accustomed smell, the *Yiddishkeit,* the Jewishness, missing. A small, heavyset black woman in a housedress and slippers stood in the center of the lobby shouting to some

52

children at play. The children were staring at us, especially at Karin; black beards were not unusual but blond hair was. We continued in, past the artifacts of my youth, the two doors I had hurriedly pushed open in my escape from school and which had later closed forever behind my dying father en route to the hospital, the stairways where I took my first cigarette drags.

I climb with Karin up to the third floor to look at the door of my old apartment. Twenty years we had lived there, my father had spent five dying there in the bedroom. Finally the door, C-10, our metal *mezzuzah* still there, ninety other *mezzuzahs* still there: Bloomgarden's, Peters', Sherman's, Cathcher's, Braverman's, Diamond's, and all the others. I explain to Karin the significance of the *mezzuzah*, a small prayer box affixed to the doorway, a covenant with God, now anachronistic, unknown and unnoticed. I smell the door—all the apartments had characteristic odors—I am hoping all the while that the door doesn't suddenly open and an eight-foot black appear, saying, "Watcha want here?" And me answering, "I'm just smelling the doorway to see if it smells the same." But it doesn't happen, and we disappear down the back stairs, me telling Karin what it's like to be a kid growing up in Brooklyn, and we're down in the lobby again like a tour group finishing up a ruin, when out of the no-bulb darkness comes this woman I recognize—Jewish, seventy at least, an atavist flowing back to my childhood, left here by her children in their frantic flight to the "Island," wandering, shuffling in her *stepsheach.* She sees us; there is a remote connection somewhere in the hind brain. She doesn't understand though, and shuffles past us like a phantom, mumbling to Karin in Yiddish, "The elevators, they make water in the elevators, the *schwartzahs.*" She *stepsheachs* on, back into the lobby—into what for her too is a void—and the blacks, they somehow understand and make room for her and let her pass.

We stood outside in front of this behemoth house that occupies one-half of a square city block, and watch several black men with chamois cloths polishing their cars. They have taken the place of the Jewish inhabitants, who used to stand in front of this house, or on warm summer nights sit on folding chairs they brought downstairs with them; the men on one side and their wives on the other, discussing, *yentering*, business and the ballgame or their kids. Through those kids such places as the Lawrence Radiation Laboratory or the Harvard Medical School were not unknown to them, and Carroll Street peaceful then, cool, a breeze coming out of Lincoln Terrace Park washing the streets, the voices absorbed by the night, and occasionally a siren interrupting the stillness.

We walked around the corner to Ford Street, where I pointed out the windows of c-10, the windows from which I eagerly watched for my father to come home from work, seeing him first from the bedroom, then from the living room; finally he would wave to me a hello. I told Karin of Bobby who used to live in the frame house across the street and who, while waiting for my father to appear, I would watch pull magazines tied to the end of a string, his large mongoloid head directing him around and around the block all day, stopping to rest in front of the Italian's house next door to his, where the Italian's dog would begin to bark and smash himself against the fence wanting a piece of Bobby who would dumbly stare at the frenzied dog and tug on his magazines as if to assure himself they were still there.

We then walked behind the house, where, as a small child who was ill and home from school, I would sit on a blanket on the steps of the back porch, which in better and earlier times was fashioned as sort of a sun deck for the mothers and their kids in carriages, 1940 white-clothed, black-belted mothers wheeling large Cadillac-like baby carriages with chrome trim in what was once a neighborhood that boasted doormen, my mother said. I remember most of all those steps in the sun, how everything would seem to melt away, the wood of the steps now splintering would be warm to the touch and pieces still covered with the green paint of the old days would catch the light—and I drew Karin close to me as if to bind her together with me in this past where everything that was complicated would uncomplicate, there in the old amnion.

I was inundating her. Giving her massive doses of myself. Showing her my past, detailing to her who I was. I pulled her to the Jewish delicatessen to have a tongue on club with a side of french fries and a Dr. Brown's Cream Soda in the still-standing Joe's Delicatessen on Utica Avenue near President Street. I had lived through two owners and the countermen gave us

a big welcome, all of them shaking hands with us. They
didn't ask me what I was doing for fear of embarrassing
me if I had "failed," but recounted the old times. We ate
our sandwiches with pure gluttony and I told Karin of
Jack's Nut Shop—where the whole neighborhood would
get "appetizing" (lox, bagels, potato, herring, and egg
salads, whitefish, dates, nuts, fancy foods, cheeses of
every type, etc.) on Sunday mornings, and describe to
her the ritual of ordering. The performer, a family man,
dressed in his sharkskin, GGG suit, his shiny temple-
black shoes, his balding head, lugubrious lips red like
the lox he was inspecting, would order with great
Napoleonic sway to the humble, white-aproned clerk—
who, lest you be deceived, also had a sharkskin outfit
but knew his role behind the counter completely. Karin
was laughing uproariously at my description. I had
never seen her so free. The show would commence, I
continued, with an authoritative "Give me," moment's
pause, "a half pound Nova," pointing to the more expensive variety of smoked salmon behind the glass—the
other customers silent, waiting their turn, watching
closely, not interrupting, recognizing the orderer's sov-
ereignty.

We laughed and laughed. And the afternoon evapo-
rated. There was time left for egg-creams at Yamo's
newspaper stand and then for Karin the race back to
Connecticut. The return trip that left me empty each
time, empty and alone.

vii

Another afternoon. Prospect Park. The great mall beside the rose garden. Still warm enough to sit comfortably on the grass. Karin telling me about Germany. About her brother and their friends. And while she talked, my own special vision of Germany appeared and tagged along with her stories. Nineteen-forty-one born, the Germany of my youth filled my elementary school notebooks. Helmets, swastikas, Messerschmitts, Panzer divisions, marched across my arithmetic, interfered with my produce and mineral maps of South America, and often, by my intense preoccupation with the rendering of a particular tank or plane, distracted me from the academic tasks at hand. But there was no real loss of education. The question of my own Jewishness was submerged beneath the art. I knew as a youth, through the careful indoctrination of my father, of anti-semitism. But in grade school, the systematic genocide of my European counterparts by the Nazis was to me simply an airplane, a tank, or a Luger pistol, shaded carefully so as to give perspective. This afternoon, on the grass, it was different. Germany sat beside me in the form of Karin—and I loved this form for I knew her to be gentle and kind—and yet her father's greatcoat was black; he was a Nazi, not simply a soldier.

Across from us on the grass danced some children, *Hasidic* children who with the blacks now populated Crown Heights, and these children danced in the clothes of their heritage—the boys in long-sleeved white shirts and suspenders, black *yarmulkes* over their close-cropped heads and long curled earlocks, the girls in frilly long-sleeved dresses, with tights to hide from sight the nakedness of their young legs, hair that would be shorn in marriage now radiant and laced with ribbons —dancing and playing no differently from other children their age. Their mothers sitting and watching, speaking quietly among themselves, no different perhaps in parental affection from any other mother, except special in this one regard—they were all stamped, marked, tattooed like beef in the stockyard or items marked down in a store, they were just human beings marked for life in a very personal, very unique way. They bore the numbers of their camps in the order of their arrival, but the script was peculiar, individualized by the SS scribe who greeted the trains, and for as many death camps as there were, and teachers who taught numbers, the tattooed sevens or threes or nines were original creations, either big or small, hurried or studied, went the numbers. And when the numbers were called—the children then bore them too—so were the lives. The *Hasidic* women wore *sheitels*, or wigs, and my eyes uncovered those wigs and saw the past, the not-so-far-away past.

I sat with Karin in silence now and stared mutely at the children—they were having so much fun—but into my mind, my head, my hole, crept death. He wasn't wearing jack boots now, but was from my own past. He was my first death—the first death I witnessed as a medical student. His heart had arrested twice in the emergency room and spontaneously recovered. He was then brought upstairs to the Cardiac Care Unit. His chart described him as a 65-year-old, white, afebrile businessman who had complained of chest pain (his own words were: "like an elephant had sat on my chest") for several hours, pain which radiated down his arm into his fingers. While in a state of terrified agitation—his heart was in shock, his body bathed in sweat—an endotracheal tube was passed with a laryngoscope against his muted struggles (his wrists were taped to the sides of the bed) down his throat so as to maintain an open airway and with which to connect him to oxygen. Fed through his nose was a "sneezo," or nasogastric catheter, which emptied his stomach contents and soon brought up quite a large amount of blood which was the product of an ulcer under stress. An arterial catheter was introduced through a brachial cut-down and an intra-aortic balloon—a narrow, 40-cc rubber device inflated by helium, which was to share the work of his heart—was passed up the femoral artery into his descending aorta. All of this was displayed on screens, of course, and the nurses and technicians monitored the screens for any irregularity in the rhythm or rate of the heart, or in the arterial pressure, or the excursions of the balloon. Intrigued and excited, I too maintained this bedside and televised vigil, and before it was over—that is, when "V-tac" or ventricular tachycardia came across the screen and the heart which has a normal rate of 75 sped up to 160 beats per minute like the engine of a race car which in this case had only one tire—it was the nurses' diagnosis that the patient was suffering from "Fat Jew," surely an untreatable malady. And when the defibrillator shock which lifted him off the bed failed to change polarities and slow down his runaway heart, and, later, could not recreate life for him at all, and after the fifteen doctors surrounded his bed, taking turns at resuscitating the failing and dying heart, pounding his chest until the ribs gave way, and rupturing the aneurysm that lay clotted and silent beneath, rolling his eyes like a window shade into the top of his head, there could no longer be any doubt of that diagnosis. It wasn't simply the spending of an exhausted man's life, it was different indeed, like the Jews who became soap, or those who became lamp shades—it was just the death of a Jew, too fat for his heart's own good.

viii

My relationship with Karin was deepening. The time spent away from one another, the nights alone, increased our wanting. Yet it could not always be arranged. There were the problems. Small ones like finding a friend to babysit. Or large ones that loomed overhead, that came with the leukemia, and over which we exerted no control save the will to live and to remain together. It would come during the night, this period of incommunicado forced by her marriage, when the incompleteness of the past was rehashed in our heads, reworked until it was understood and made palatable, and then held until morning for reconnection. When her leukemic crises came, my daytime calls to her home went unanswered, and then suddenly, out of the blue, I would hear from her, from the hospital, a new one now in a place kept secret from me—she never wanted me to see her ill—and a weak voice, one unmistakeably close to death, would enquire about the weather outside. Was the sun coming into our room? And the room we shared became empty for me as the grave during those times. I was never more alone. When my own words weren't enough encouragement, when I could no longer play the fool, or the prophet, or the lunatic, and coerce her into some small degree of happiness, I would resort to the words of others. I shall never forget the effect William Kotzwinkle's *The Fanman* had on her. The exploits of the overcoat that went to the Bronx, Puerto Rican music, Jamaican meatbuns and the rooftop Hawkman took her out of blackness.

Having escaped a crisis, she would spend weeks recuperating, and our relationship was then entirely telephonic. Through the wires. Brooklyn on the one end and Connecticut on the other. It was a transfusion for both of us, invested in each some life, or at least an excuse for living, and made our lives spend more easily. It was the relationship through the wire, though, that tugged at the reality. How much of me did she really know? Surely only my better side—she never woke beside me in the morning, my breath never stank, I was almost always supportive. And she was for me the same. Perhaps it was this separation that encouraged our growth, though other forces were involved, forces that went unnamed and weren't accorded recognition.

Then remission. Recovery without cure. She was back with me, setting up the card table in the living room and spreading out a gourmet dinner she had prepared at home, opening the wine, clinking the glasses, being once again together, lying afterwards in the late afternoon sun, and forcing out from our minds the inevitable departure. "Do you love me?" I asked. She smiled but didn't answer. "Do you love me?" I repeated. "Please don't ask me that," she snapped. "What more do you want? You know I must always return home." "I want you. You. For myself," I said.

Outside. Walking her to her car. To the capsule that would deliver her to Connecticut and her life there. A life no less real. With a daughter she loved. And a husband who could no longer support his role as her father, teach her a practical arithmetic with which to order her life. To the parties. The playgrounds. The friends. And the books. The novels which I told her to read and which connected her to me like the line of a fishing reel.

Of her feelings then I offer her first letter to me as evidence, as evidence of her intentions, of the promise of our love.

Michael,

I have a strong desire for your small shoulders, your crazy humor, and your slightly astonished water blue eyes. Do you believe that I sometimes think I must burst with desire to be with you in the same room? Each time when I leave you, a piece of me remains behind. How long do you think I will be able to go when my legs entangle you, when my hands caress you; but, here, on the other side, nobody has yet realized their absence. Perhaps one could construct a body and leave that instead. In this world they don't ask for much, the things built into that body could be simple, its functions uncomplicated, and I could just fly together with you to the sun. They say it is very warm there. Sometimes, I cannot comprehend that I met you, just as a beggar who is locked in a fight with death and who finds a golden coin, a coin he cannot spend anymore, but still has time to admire and to love this treasure.

another mad admirer

ix

The Negro in the laminar-flow room suddenly awoke
from his coma, they told me later. His future now was
certain. It had been cast again. In the cells. His longings
were ignored, his childhood influenced no one. He tried
to make sense of his surroundings. The tube coming out
of his throat. His thigh wrapped in bandages. And then,
and then, his heart exploded. Quarts of blood coming out
of his mouth and nose. He started, as if to leave. But
remained, in an almost sitting position. His finger pointing to his throat. To signal the source. His eyes bulged.
Then rolled. The blood soaked the sheets and poured off
the bed. In waves. And the audience watched,
transfixed. Helpless. Speechless. For when the heart
bursts there is no turning back. No second try. No
Hindu. The puddles beneath the bed were sopped up
with paper towels, the floor mopped. His tube was
removed and his gaping mouth was taped shut with
nearly two feet of adhesive. And his eyes, which had

steadfastly remained open, were now taped closed. He was enveloped in a plastic body bag. His head beneath the knot.

With the help of a sedative, Lukash had remained asleep throughout the leave-taking. After writing the death certificate, I went in to examine the take. Lukash slept like a baby, the only clue to dysfunction was the whistling sound his lungs made as they expelled air. On his forehead was the black skin graft. It was wrinkled and was beginning to show signs at the borders of sloughing off. Pus was appearing at the breathing holes. It didn't look good. Not only had the Negro died, but now his donation to science was dying too. Lukash snored, and it seemed to me that the black patch slipped forward on his forehead.

X

We were dispossessed by time and by *minestrone* soup that found us in a friend's apartment on the upper West Side. In the top bunk of a double-bunk bed where I turned her around until her ass pointed skywards and attempted to enter her. And the dam broke. Tears streaming out of her eyes, no noise though, just tears. "Don't do that—it's so degrading." I apologized. I apologized one hundred times. But it was no use. "Do you want to pay me?" she cried. She thought "perhaps" we shouldn't see each other again. That it was too much. The secrecy. The two lives. I persisted, I tried to talk her out of it, the ending that is. I was unprepared—in shock —it wasn't a matter of her ass—it was the other mining —and how deep it was getting—nearing a vein—a vein of commitment. She stood in the apartment's tiny bathroom, making up her face, her Connecticut face, and I stood behind her in the doorway and was captured with her in the mirror. My head above hers. We drove back in my car to where she was parked at the 168th Street entrance to the Henry Hudson Parkway, and tears came freely from both of us now.

I refused to believe it was over. It couldn't be. I wouldn't allow it. But who was I in all of this? She had a family—a child. A death notice. And me. I was a skin doctor who had escaped the Institute. Who had opened his cage and sought freedom and nourishment outside. But from whom did I seek it, from a person who could less afford it than myself? Was I giving or taking? Had I turned the cancer around so thoroughly that I was sucking on its teat and refusing to be weaned? When she vanished into the bridge traffic—I followed the car until it disappeared from my sight—I felt that a part of me had been ripped away. And it hadn't been torn by death either. Just ourselves. I started walking back to the apartment, leaving my car. Three miles back, stretching the umbilicus with each step, but unable to break it.

Before me lay Harlem. The great gateway on 125th Street, St. Nicholas Terrace, Lennox Avenue, and the life in the lights. The roar of the life. The expenditure of energy. A roaring artery beside the quiet vein of Riverside Drive. The Riverside Drive of Columbia with its gentle transition from old Jews to young ones who were lined up for the mammoth apartments facing the Hudson that vacated with death. I veered off into Harlem. Into parts unknown. Into the Black World. And I walked with a certain seriousness of purpose, a certain craziness, you might say, that protected me from harassment. Have you ever seen 109th Street with its glass and its garbage strewn on the street, the brown paper bags burst like the hulks of spent bombs and the buildings gutted like Dresden? And in all this chaos people surviving. Surviving by the will to live and, sometimes, the terrible will to kill and die. The shoes of Harlem, the heels, and the colors, and the cars, and the hats, and the lips now dry, now wet, the stores of 125th Street and the Jewish dinette sets, the chicken shacks, the windows barred, the barber shops, the crazy skin doctor walking through this, trying to put together the pieces of his own life in this dissonance—the music blaring, deafening, the groups of people on the corner, tall, powerful, black leather coats, moving, angling, swaying, hustling, bending with the gracefulness of saplings, careening, screaming, wailing sirens, project houses mountain tall and the roar in the incinerator vault as garbage falls free to explode ten stories below.

For two weeks we kept radio silence; I was the first to break. I picked up the phone and it shook in my hand with fear and excitement. The fear was egotistical, it cast me as too important a figure in her life and thereby capable of irrevocably damaging it, destroying its precarious balance. To argue against this, I saw her as the George Washington Bridge spanning two states with its mighty steel girders—no Galloping Gerdy—all the molecules seated, the lattices undisturbed and in place. The excitement—it was met in kind by her voice as she answered the phone, a voice without reproach. She told me that if I hadn't called that day, she would have the next day, that she wanted to from the start, but was afraid.

xi

It was after Lukash's black forehead had sloughed off completely and was found in his sheets that I went to visit him. "Listen Doc," he began, "I sure am sorry about that black skin coming off. I knew you really wanted it to stick. You know I tried my best."

"Don't be crazy Tony, I know you didn't lose the graft on purpose, and I appreciate your giving me the chance to try. Something's gone wrong in the experiment, I've had grafts like this take before. We're missing something, perhaps something really simple."

"Maybe it was on accounta the guy being colored. Do you think that made any difference? My wife said . . ."

"Tony, you don't understand, that's precisely why we used a black donor. Because it would make a difference, be genetically incompatible."

There were any number of reasons that could have contributed to the failure. An unnoticed change in the technique involved in grafting the skin onto Lukash. A viral infection in the tissue. A sudden change in temperature during the refrigeration process. The news of our failure, however, was not to be contained within the walls of the flow room. My colleagues at the Institute, many of whom were angered by my immediate appointment as a Member, were quick to spread the word. By week's end even the Xerox operator knew about our plight and had expressed his doubt. Inevitably the news reached the Director, who appointed a recent post-doctorate in the Institute to set up a laboratory in remote quarters to duplicate on basic models my earlier findings. In this state of trust and faith I was expected to continue my own work. To ignore the bloodhounds at the other end of the building. To be guided by only one principle, fidelity. The truth of the matter is that, by this time, I didn't care. My life was no longer contained by science. I no longer lived alone in a test tube. My own life demanded more than the ability to heal, to discover. Yet my relationship with Karin was not without those elements. Nevertheless, a junior associate, who was taking charge of our own replication of the basic model studies in my increasingly longer absences from the laboratory, was able to demonstrate in two of six experiments where technical adjustments were made, successful grafts in five hamsters sixty to seventy-five days after transplantation. For a while this finding, which was published, bought time from the Director. Time spent by others.

In Britain, Volner was reported to have said, after his own failure at validation, that the only way his group would believe my findings was if they personally saw a white man with a black patch. Our old demonstration hamster, one of the original remaining, was black with a white tuft. The doubters and disparagers were quick to point out that the white patch may not have been the result of a successful transplant between unrelated animals, but may have been a cross between a black and white animal. Or perhaps the animals, unbeknownst to us, were, in fact, related. All of this was possible with white patches on black hamsters. But impossible genetically in the reverse.

The presentation Volner wanted to see, a white man with a black patch, could be derived only from skin grafting, and with Lukash's graft shed, it no longer existed. A deadline was set, Volner's next meeting with the Board. The atmosphere of the Institute was electric, like the arena in Rome. The professors were pushing each other out of the way for a glimpse of the struggle, and it wasn't success they were rooting for, it was failure and downfall. Cancer was just the football.

xii

After a long period of telephone contact, the inevitable —Karin had another leukemic crisis. About a month later we met in the early afternoon in a nearly deserted county park in Westchester. She had brought along a bottle of wine and two glasses, and we huddled together under a plaid blanket beside the pond. We spoke very little and felt very much. She wanted to know whether I had noticed that she was losing her eyelashes from the treatment she was taking, and whether the false eyelashes she wore "bothered me." I told her my position on eyelashes. Joined once again we welded together beneath that blanket, and as we skipped our thoughts across the water, surprised at the absence of ripples, we were never closer. There was no need to talk, talking was for the telephone. It was a victory celebration of sorts, the winning of her last bout with leukemia and the reassertion of our will to remain together. There should have been sun that day, but instead it was gray and cold. Yet there was no warmer, no more comfortable space than inside our blanket.

∙∙∙
xiii

Fifty milligrams of Librium and I'm ready to continue. If it were only just the science. The skin. How eloquent I could become on the subject of transplanted skin. The experts from Washington—the National Institutes of Health, the National Cancer Institute, Volner himself sent a deputy, along with his philosophy of science, the Calculus of Discovery. The Purity of the Hypothesis. The Purity of the Scientific Fraternity—the Brotherhood of International Scientists—A.F.L.–C.I.O. One mistake though, some dirty underwear that escapes the hamper without permission, and you're out. A trip to Bayonne, Hackensack, where auto chassis—bodies of reputation—are decimated into smithereens by the press. I'm escaping ahead of myself here. The neurons are dieseling. Let me try to recover.

The eloquence of transplantation. How important the skin. How very important. The site committee from Washington: "Tell us, Dr. Halbgewachs, about your program." The experts are seated around the board table, mostly from the Midwest, state-university trained, color coded ties, handkerchiefs, shirts, uneasy this morning because the clowns in the General Accounting Office put them into a hotel on 42nd Street that doubles as a massage parlor. So they're here early, way ahead of schedule, too bashful to talk to one another. It seems the pimps woke them up about four in the morning, some screaming in the hallways. They're wolfing down donuts and coffee—all set up nicely by the Institute—to go with my slide collection, a trip across the country: from skin to skin, limbus to limbus, black hamster to white hamster, cadaver eye to rabbit, and black man to white. In Kodachrome. First though, Vietnam, to get them into the mood—the senior N.I.H. official farting now, the odor of donuts.

"Vietnam, gentlemen, as you know (Yes, we are all gentlemen—white lab coats, you know, what's a little My Lai between good ol' boys—the head of the delegation is named Orville, he is whiter than white), produced more burn victims than ever before. While at the Army Burns Research Bureau at Fort Sam Houston, gentlemen, I saw and treated those men. In many cases three-quarters of the body's surface area denuded by Napalm (Sugar, you know, Marca Registrada Dow Chemical—just a little careless Orville, trying to scald the gooks or their kids on their way to school—sort of like a Variation on a Theme by Nagasaki except they fell short—the bombardier's faulty instruments sold at the Shenandoah Bridge Club, or just his ignorance of coordinate geometry, and the Sugar, it was just right, syrupy like Dow said—it clung until all the skin burnt away and it didn't matter that the kid's name was O'Connell and he was from Virginia, it took away the skin regardless, until there was nothing holding back the liquid and we had a waterfall on our hands gentlemen—you gentle men of science—the body fluids cascading off the bed in sheets, like Niagara, and the electrolytes gone forever onto the floor), and no adequate mode of treatment, just the piecemeal transfer of one length of skin from the thigh to the chest, another from the buttock, and, if the patient has enough skin to spare and is still alive without his electrolytes or hasn't succumbed to septicemia, we find a new piece to patch. Now, contrary to Robinson and Prendergast, we have performed experiments that document considerable extension of adult human whole-skin viability after refrigeration, viability ultimately confirmed by permanent autologous transplantation. Moreover, we now have both hamster and human data showing that donor antigens maintain their integrity during refrigeration, and persist after subsequent allo-geneic and xenogeneic transplantation without rejec-tion. Projector please."

I show them a black soldier, obviously a burn victim, with white patches of skin grafted in a jig-saw design—tiny islands in a sea of blood—on his denuded body. They stare at the slide, nervous at first, then they begin to titter, to laugh, imagine, a nigger with white skin. Next a guinea pig with a cornea from a human corpse. They have questions though, after all they represent

78

the great American public: "Where can I get a pair of white shoes and belt like Joe's in this burg?" or "Hell, can you imagine the folks back home when they find out we're transplanting white skin onto colored." Actually, they just present little advertisements of themselves, prepared for the occasion in advance, some obviously having nothing to do with the presentation at all but recited anyway, as a matter of course.

What do I owe this body of Science? These so-called colleagues who now demand my honor. I saw what I saw. Their only complaint is that they failed to stone me early enough. The line has formed now, the screaming begun, who saw the falsehood first; we knew, we observed correctly, we are the guardians of the faith. But what about their own hands, their own fingers, into whose ass, whose mouth are they stuck now? Forget their operating rooms where the blood the public never sees bathes the walls; what about their kitchens, their bedrooms? Yes, I plead guilty, but not to this lesser charge. Let me continue to tell you of my attempt at loving Karin and the real crime will become obvious.

xiv

Danger crept in. Danger to my own body. Karin's husband suspected something was wrong. He was often unable to reach her at home in the afternoon, and when she was convalescing, he sometimes couldn't get through for hours. Where was she going? Who was she calling? Karin managed somehow to allay his fears. But he wasn't entirely convinced, so he hired a private detective, she told me, to find me and rearrange my anatomy. An ex-Embassy Marine who had met her at a ski resort in Austria, Brian was no stranger to violence. In fact he had killed. Schoolyard fights and clinical ineptitude were my only brutalities to the body, so I called a friend who had some experience. "Get a gun," he advised me, "and don't use it until he steps into your apartment, otherwise you'll be screwed." So I bought a 9mm Browning automatic with a clip that held thirteen bullets, hollow-points that mushroomed on impact. There was nothing toylike about this weapon; it could pass only for the real thing. It was ugly, incredibly ugly, and possessing it made me physically uncomfortable. I was never sure if I would use it, though, and when I daydreamed about the possibility of confrontation I never forsook the potential for conciliation. A quiet talk between the concerned principals, Karin, the subject of the controversy, not present. He and I would part as friends. I suppose this fantasy could be attributed to guilt, to reason, to cowardice. Certainly, I felt that I wanted her more than I feared death. After all, she, and I and death were old buddies. We were veterans—like her husband. And decorated too. But there was a certain attraction in holding this pistol, in firing it at the range and in reeling in the target—a silhouette of a human torso now punctured by the spectra of thirteen rounds perfectly found in the vital organs of the unknown form.

We were very careful in the weeks that followed. Alibis were developed. Friends were taken into the conspiracy. The private detective, or the threat of one, disappeared. We roamed New York City, the streets, the stores, museums, the restaurants, Prospect Park, the Zoo, the Jersey Palisades. And we merged completely. I thought there was no doubt left in my mind that I wanted to be with her always and Karin told me she felt the same. There were periods, though, spent in the exercise of reason, which like dross surfaced to disturb our doubtlessness.

"My medical costs, you know, every time I get sick . . . Brian has spent already eighteen thousand dollars a year to keep me alive. He sold our house." She still had loyalty, but it was to a lover and a ring of long ago. Before he had changed. Before they had both changed. "And Molly, you know I love her." I did know. I knew how much she loved her. And there was the guilt—the adultery—and the story she told me of an episode in boarding school.

Her father the General had sent his daughters to a convent school to be educated by the church. The students lived together in dormitories, the sisters and novices in another building. Well, it seemed that one of the novices had second thoughts about her vows and had expressed them to the school doctor, a young Arab, who often amused the girls hanging like apples from the tree outside his window, by masturbating into a porno magazine. And the apples had witnessed other acts of this school doctor as well, like when he treated the novice, and soon the whole school knew. "So one day," Karin said, "we were all seated at dinner, about one hundred of us, prayers had been said, when in walked this novice, late. She never really knew until then, you know, she never knew that we all knew. And everyone in the dining hall stopped eating and looked at her, stared at her in silence, but she sat down anyway. Then, about five minutes later, she got up and ran out of the room. They found her later. She had hung herself from a beam in her room."

This story was not without other meaning. Karin, too, feared being found out, she feared the public denunciation by her husband and his family, and she terribly feared the prospects of her own judgment, the consequences of living as she pleased without debt to either life or death. In the igloo of the whorehouse she had resigned herself to death, assaulted herself, mortified herself. By this refrigeration she was able to escape her daughter's lovehold, a stranglehold that made her promise each and every night she would be alive the next morning. Alive when the doctors and the leukocytes were still unsure. And me, how did I fit into all of this? It was simple. I took out my ball-peen hammer and began to make chinks in the igloo, chop away pieces of the ice, let in some of the sun; and I did it for very selfish reasons, reasons that I now fully admit. I did this in order to breathe, in order to fill my asphyxiated lungs with air—with life. But the igloo began to melt, slowly at first and then faster with each missing brick, until the figure encased in the dome stood free and alone in the puddle melted around her and once again faced the prospect of death, of leaving loves behind, and living under the axe. But of all these, what she feared most was her own judgment, her own punishment.

We talked of her getting a separation, of going to Germany and speaking with her brother the psychiatrist, someone she was close to and trusted. We spoke of meeting in Germany. And we dreamt. "But what about Molly?" she asked. "Could I take my daughter?" And shamefacedly I sat down by the hole in the wall beside her. I sat down in the puddle of melted ice until the seat of my pants was soaked through and I appeared incontinent. The effect of our love possessed us, the tools of its emancipation surrounded us lying scattered about, partially submerged in the puddle. But tenaciously we clung to the chains, unsure, afraid, like slaves suddenly made free.

XV

Illness was quick to reoccupy its place in the hierarchy of our thoughts. Karin suffered another attack and was again hospitalized. She wouldn't tell me where and I only heard from her when she had gathered enough strength to write. Her letter contained a poem. I include it here.

Geliebter Michael,
you'll probably can guess where I'm stuck, but I should be out next week. It is rather difficult for me to call (I am wired with life voltage) and the nurses conspired to keep me in bed (I pinned the centerfold of Cosmopolitan in the nurse lounge and got an seventy-three-year-old patient drunk). The view from my room is lousy (no sun) and my room-mate prays aloud, hereby attracting a mild-mannered, disgustingly pink faced "Rabe" (speak minister) who drowns me in his damned blessings. I am crazy about you!

My whole life is
        So demanding
I have to be
        Polite and
        Respectable
I must never
        Step out of
          Place or
          act
          Superior
When
I hurt
I should ride it
        And
        Pretend
There is no
        Pain
        Why?
I want to
        Act
        Silly and
        Throw
        Fits and
        Cry and
        Run
          Wild in the streets
I am
    Sick of
        Holding things
        In and
Being conventional.
        One day

I intend to
> break loose
>> And
>>> Blow
this whole fucking world out of place
>>>>> Karin

Some days I would attempt to sleep all day, wishing only that her voice would awaken me. Instead came the increasingly dismal progress reports from my laboratory and the unexpected decision from the National Cancer Institute not to award my work a grant in aid. I wasn't disturbed by the news; I wanted nothing more than Karin.

What a device the telephone—how careful the measure and worth of each word without the face of the voice on the other side. When she finally called I was delivered, but I wanted more—to know what effect my words, my demands, had on her, to know whether she was smiling, crying, angry, or in pain. "Just weak," she would tell me. We spoke of the future, of Europe, where I had never been, and, perhaps, of meeting there. Where we would go, and what we would do. A lot was left out of these discussions, though. The Philadelphia chromosome to be smuggled across the border was never mentioned. Her husband and his expected unwillingness to let this happen also escaped. But never did I fully express my own doubts—doubts that remained most times undefined; yet when they surfaced, they brought forth considerable anxiety.

Her daughter, for example, became a problem. I wanted no third party. And the fear of doomsday—my fear, not hers—couldn't be expressed. So the coward that I am, I remained silent, steadfast, and became for her an anchor of certainty. But the anchor was rusty. Not to be trusted. Links might open up and she would slip away. I ignored the issue, like I have ignored the skin, and left her alone with the burden of decision. Not that I didn't tell her always that I loved her and wanted her, and even expressed reluctance—almost invisibly—about including her daughter in our plans. And when there were no more words, when the desire overcame our fluency, we simply held the receivers to our heads without them, and thoughts passed as vibrations between us. And the vibrations, they did wonders, for simple connection was the most important element of all.

We spoke again the following week and she reiterated her desire to end her marriage. She thought that if she moved into her own apartment with her daughter—if Brian allowed her to—it would be an easier transition. We would still have some independence—each a place to retire to if necessary, a place in which to hide. She told me that she had written a letter to her brother in Germany about meeting with him soon to discuss what was happening, but she was vague about the specifics. She had much improved and would be discharged soon. Her leukemia was remarkable in that respect; it would bring her near to death and then, almost miraculously, there would be a spontaneous recovery.

Part Three

i

Karin was discharged from the hospital two weeks later, but she wasn't to make it all the way home. She had taken a cab from the hospital and had had the driver stop across the street from her apartment house. She got out of the cab, she said, and saw a small boy trying, with much difficulty, to cross a bicycle that was two heads taller than himself. So she put down her suitcase and began to help him take the bike across the street, when from around the corner, skidding on two wheels, a car came racing down the street and knocked her and the bike high into the air. The boy had already made it safely across. Karin landed on her head against the curb.

An ambulance took her to a local hospital. The call that I finally got came from her there two weeks later. She had been unconscious for some time. She spoke haltingly, the receiver continuously falling out of her hand. I scarcely breathed during those silences. I saw her being taken away from me and I was powerless to do anything. I felt her pain in my own body as she described hers, and was choked with tears. Then the receiver fell and thunked loudly on the floor. "Karin," I yelled. "Karin, are you all right?" There was no answer. I stayed on the line for fifteen minutes. Still no answer. Finally the phone was hung up, placed in its cradle by someone who didn't recognize the other side of things. What could I do? Had she fallen out of bed? Was she still alive? She had never told me her married name and she had certainly been admitted under it. I couldn't call every hospital in southern Connecticut and describe her. So instead of going to the laboratory, I forced myself to stay in the apartment, pacing like an animal in its cage, waiting for the call. It was not to come for several days.

I left occasionally to shop for food and to walk in Prospect Park. It was getting colder now and the park was practically empty of people. Six hundred acres large, once inside it you could never tell you were in Brooklyn. It is a beautiful park, with paved walks lined by trees, and benches placed in shady nooks. It holds a thousand surprises, at least, which only the old folks and kids who roam it daily in the warmer months are free to discover. There are old statues, hills in what was once called Flatbush, labyrinthine paths, great meadows that suddenly come into view, a Quaker Cemetery where General George W. Wingate (a Revolutionary War hero and the namesake of my high school) is buried, a zoo, a lake, and many memories for me over the years. As a boy I took refuge in this park on early weekend mornings and usually would make my way to the zoo where the bears were being fed huge sandwich loaves of white bread for breakfast.

On the afternoon Karin and I first made love in my apartment we later went outside, Karin putting on my oversized and stolen Harvard D. of A. sweat shirt which draped over her jeans, and we raced into the park our hands locked together. That run was the finest in my life. I was for the first time tied to someone I genuinely loved, someone who connected me to earth.

How romantic all of this, you must think—the mayonnaise running in gobs out of the jar—but walking alone down the same hill we had run down together brought home the loneliness that was overpowering me. It wasn't Karin who was dying any longer, it was me. She had resuscitated me; she filled me with life.

Once, I let myself loose from the shackle of the telephone and escaped out the other side of the park, the side that led to my old neighborhood a mile away. I had always paid special attention to the Crown Heights sidewalks in my years as a wanderer. The area's peculiar mix of cement laced with flecks of mica connected me to the old times. I walked lost in thought, as if wading through the pavement square after square, until I arrived at Lincoln Terrace Park and the endless row of benches that faced my old apartment house and block. I sat down where I remembered Mr. Berman used to sit. He was a writer on the *Forward*, who because of poor health, was forced to retire early and would sit bundled in a navy blue overcoat with hat and scarf, warm day or cold, on these same benches. I never knew much more than that he was a Yiddish writer and ill, but his gentleness attracted me to him and I always spent some time chatting with him if he was sitting outside. He would patiently listen to my remonstrations and always say something that let me feel better—perhaps it was just his smile that punctuated his ever-present cough. Every winter seemed to be his last and, finally, one winter he died. The neighborhood soon followed.

I stared at our house across the street and dreamt. *I lay again on the American Flyer sled and pretended that the hardwood floor was snow and that I was sleighing down Ford Street, my face in the wind. But there was no wind in our apartment. It was airtight with rags stuffed between the windows and the sills. It was hermetically sealed from life. My mother liked it like that. Air carried germs. Life carried germs. One was better off without such air, without such a life. My mother had retired so far from life that she no longer seemed alive herself. Only her breasts appeared alive as they swung around to indict me. "What are you doing on the floor?" she whined. "Get up or you'll catch cold." My mother saw to it that I didn't catch cold. And also that I went to the bathroom. It was as if she had a pact with my kidneys. "Do you have to go to the bathroom?" she would whine. A thousand times a day. Until I was drained, flaccid, and on the floor. "Get off the floor, I told you. Can't you hear."*

Twelve years of excusions through these rooms make an expert. One becomes an intimate. Of the anoxia, the smells, the cracks, the colors, the creaks, and the feel of its surfaces. And after the intimacy comes the contempt. For the walls become confining and the pictures of the outside through its windows invite an escape. A connection. But there is none. There is a lock. And the need for permission. For outside there is life. And that is dangerous. For a boy. And his mother.

The father is a clerk. A chief clerk. But being the chief doesn't mean much to the father. Only to the son. The father sits down at the small kitchen table and eats. The breasts serve. And the son watches. The father's mouth opens and the shovel enters. Faster and faster. Like they ate in years past. In the caves. Of Auschwitz. The boy laughs at a thought passing through the three rooms. Suddenly his father is standing. Saliva is dripping from his mouth. He has grabbed a meatball from off his plate and stares with murder at his son. The mother is pressed with fear against the sink. The meatball is hurled. It explodes against the boy's face. The father's hands are stretched out for the boy's throat. He lifts the boy up out of his chair and smashes him against the kitchen pipe. Again and again. The mother tries to intervene but is shoved away and cursed. In that second, the boy escapes the hands of his father. Into the bathroom, locking the door. He is safe. He glances at the mirror to assure himself of that. There is screaming outside.

The words are repeated. "The stinking bastard. I'll kill him."

The bathroom is familiar to the boy. Its surfaces are old friends. And while on its seat, its sink becomes a stage. A theatre. And he is the director. He arranges the scenes and moves the characters. At times it's a battlefield for the plastic soldiers, or a desert or arctic highway for the khaki tanks and jeeps and ambulances with red crosses. And sometimes, very often actually, it becomes a prison with watchtowers of gleaming faucets, whose subterranean cells can be flooded with water at the warden's whim. Drowning all the prisoners. All the life.

The bathroom floor is tiled. Hexagonal. And white. His eyes are captured by the tiles. One attached to another. On top and on bottom and at either side. He is absorbed by the floor, by the geometry. And by nothing else. The screams can no longer enter the room. The tile becomes a screen. And on the screen the boy sees the blood vessels projected by his eyes. He sees the bugs sailing across the aqueous, enlarged many times. He follows their movements. Their voyages seem endless. They float joyously, maneuvering past obstacles in their path. He is caught up in their freedom. Ten minutes later his eyes refocus on the tiles. He can hear no sound in the apartment. He studies the walls that closely surround him, the shower head, the curtains, and the dusty scale. It's his room, his fortress. And should he, in the course of a siege, have to do his business, he's safe here.

And then the front door slams shut. He hopes that his father has gone out. He is frightened. His mother is knocking on the door. "You can come out now. He's left. It's all right. It's all right. He's left." Cautiously, he opens the door and stares at his mother. She has been crying. Her hair is disarranged. There is a yellow-red mark on her arm. He grabs for her and she pulls him against her. Her hand is in his hair. And his sobs are muffled by her body.

She watches him undress for bed. He knows that he'll be safe now. Because of the Shema. The Shema Yisroel. *His mother kisses him goodnight and puts out the light. She is back in the kitchen. He can hear her washing the dishes.*

He pushes the covers off and stands up on the bed. The pajamas are tied tight around his waist. He feels the cord against his skin as he walks to the pillow. He is now facing the east wall. He bends down and takes a yarmulke *from underneath the pillow and puts it on his head. And he prays:* "Shema yisroel adonoi elohaynoo, adonoi airchud." *He beats his chest and bends his knees as he recites the words. The words that keep him alive. The words, which if he forgets to recite each night, his father says will kill him. For the Hebrew God is a jealous god, his father says, and will not even spare a boy.*

My neck spastically jerked as my head fell forward and I found myself in the now-darkened park. Looking behind me again and again to make sure I wasn't being followed, I hurriedly made my way home.

ii

Karin called. We talked about the vulnerability of the brain. She had taken quite a beating plus endured some painful diagnostic procedures but was faring well now it seemed. Although bleeding in the brain can be insidious, and *they* were going to keep an eye on her. We talked and joked, skirted reality. After all, wasn't this really *too* much, to get out of one hospital and into another the very same day?

"I must really be lucky," she said, her words formed in her German mouth taking on an even more impacted meaning for me.

"Yes, you are really lucky. We both are. Consider the weather outside. Cold. Miserable. We're both inside and occupied. You with your head and me with mine."

"Brian is going to take the guy who hit me to court and sue him. He called to see how I was and apologized, the nurse told me. I really don't want to sue him, but Brian says we'll win, that I deserve it. Maybe he doesn't have any money though. But Brian says he's got to have insurance."

Where am I? I asked. What is all of this? This never-ending woe. How fucking much can we, she, they, it take? How much more? The equanimity with which she accepted all of this—she wasn't even mad at the bastard who nearly killed her. Had she already been stoned, or did she expect more of a beating? She once told me of her older sister who was retarded as a result of a bout with meningitis as a child. Karin thought that *she* had given her sister the meningitis—her mother had accused her of transferring the "germ" in soiled underwear. Like a catcher she squatted at the plate. Taking each pitch, one after the other—first the spitball, then the knuckleball—all barreling in, one after the other.

"Write me," she said, "write me a letter. Make it sexy."

"I can't write letters," I protested.

"Yes, you can, you're a crazy poet, 'half mad, half saint, he roamed the countryside.' " She gave me the address—a small Catholic hospital in Greenwich. I told her I would write.

How to write a "sexy letter." I tried my best. But the mail wasn't fast enough, so I decided to bring it to her myself. I would get it to her somehow. Seeing her was impossible because Brian was often there, so I would *act* by delivering the letter myself to the hospital.

There is great ritual when Catholics fall ill, I discovered. I had never been in a Catholic hospital before, although of course I had treated Catholics. But in the

Michael Breslow

vestments of Science. Here were nuns in starched white nurse's habits, holy pictures, statues, and the visitors themselves. Working people for the most part, in white socks, discussing the varieties of illness. And beneath the ironed shirts were the muscular arms of workers, some with tattoos, and I imagined myself being caught red-handed with the letter—the "sexy letter"—that I was en route to deliver. The Jew uncovered and himself delivered to his just desserts. I was afraid of discovery, but I wanted the letter to get through, to be held by her the day she had asked for it, to be the "poet" she took me for. And beneath Christ on the cross, which appeared again and again in the hallway, I saw in my mania a sign that pointed to "Chaplain's Office."

For a Jew to enter to enter the chaplain's office is no easy task. Was it to be like a confessional, would I admit to adultery and ask forgiveness, would the chaplain remain unmoved by my story, my mission, and instead have me taken to the main lobby where under the anemic form of the King of the Jews I would be beaten to death by white socks? Or should I appear the unremitting professional man, the Doctor, who on a confidential consultation had to deliver an important deliberation that must be hidden under the cloak of secrecy? "You chaplains are above the law, are you not?" My R.A.F. insignia gleaming in the light. "I have been asked by the minister to deliver this note. . ." The fact that it was a "sexy" letter didn't even occur to me. That I was asking a priest in his sacred role to deliver an aphrodisiac.

Gently, he asked me to sit down. Warmly, he listened

100

to my urgency about delivering the letter. And with great assurance he told me that he would get the letter to her. I had accomplished my mission, though the lobby convinced me that it would be foolhardy to try and see her, that a battle scene was the last thing she needed. Was it altruism or was it the white socks? I believe now that there were no rational decisions made then, that reality had been transcended long ago, and, that, perhaps, ever being in actual physical touch with her again had escaped as well.

It wasn't that the priest had failed his part of the operation. She had gotten the letter, but after she read it and had fallen asleep, a nurse found it while changing her sheets and thinking it was worthy of safekeeping gave it to Karin's husband.

I called the next day and was told by the switchboard that she had been transferred and couldn't receive any calls. I didn't know what to think anymore; so I didn't. A half-hour later I called as a physician and was told by the charge nurse that she was in "good" health, hadn't been transferred to a surgical bed, but had been put "under observation."

iii

Confronting her with the letter as she lay in the hospital bed again bound to the never-ending I-V drips, Brian demanded to know who the writer was. What he was. How long she had known him. How big his cock was. And finally, she said, when she could no longer take it —take the beating he gave her as he fully realized his loss—she told him that if he didn't stop, she would jump out of the window. Take her life. He never doubted her seriousness. He spoke to the attending neurologist and she was transferred to psychiatry.

"They have me locked up in a psycho ward. Brian made the doctor do it. What can I do? How can I get out? It's locked!" she panicked.

"Don't worry," I not too easily offered. "I'll get you out. You can't be held against your will."

Her cries punctuated the call; I had never heard her in more despair. She had always been a prisoner, but now there were bars. And nurses who carefully examined both sides of a story, then checked the chart for the diagnosis and the verdict. She was filled with terror—of the people who surrounded her, walked by her like zombies loaded with Thorazine, and of her loss of liberty that her husband so easily took away. I told her all that I would do to free her—I would consult a colleague who was a psychiatrist at the Institute and get his advice, and if that wasn't enough I would go to court. My energy, later able to effect nothing, seemed to bring her down, calm her.

I made an appointment to see the Institute's psychiatrist. We knew each other slightly from meetings and site visits. "There's nothing you can do. The law is with her husband and doctors. If after awhile she isn't released and continues to demand her freedom, she—but not you—can retain a lawyer to go to court to obtain it. The fact of the matter is, you are *nobody* in this case. Nobody to the medical authorities involved, or to the law." He reassured me that I had done all I could, and being a coward at heart I went no further. I didn't bang on the bars outside, I didn't find her husband and beat his brains to a pulp, but stood in Brooklyn my feet sunk in cement and did nothing. Yet I imagined what the loss of freedom she now suffered was like, that she was surrounded by lunatics and their ravings. At times I vowed to get even, I imagined killing her husband and stealing her away, but in the end remained isolated from any action except in thought.

She described all of the patients and the routine of the ward to me in her next call, and was even in a good humor. She had been assured by her doctor (the neurologist treating her) that she would be out in a few days. She demonstrated health, it seems, by getting involved with ward activities, consoling other patients, encouraging them, helping the nurses. "There is a rabbi on the ward and I was sitting next to him at dinner and we were having soup, so I remembered what you had told me about the difference between a *schlemiel* and a *schlemazel.*"

"What is the difference?" I asked.

"The *schlemiel* spills soup on his shirt and the *schlemazel* on his pants. Right? So I asked the rabbi if he knew the difference. He stared at me as if I was crazy. Here was a blond *shicksa* in a crazy ward asking *him* the difference between a *schlemiel* and a *schlemazel.*" We both laughed. What a welcome relief. It actually seemed as if an end were in sight, some light at the end of the tunnel.

"We're going to the movies tonight, almost everyone on the ward. Can you imagine, a busload of mental patients going to the movies."

"What's the picture?" I asked.

"I don't know, but it probably has a special rating—so that it can't offend *anybody*. . . . As soon as I'm out we'll get together and go away, all right? Will you wait?"

"Yes," I answered, "I'll wait."

iv

She never phoned me again. For two weeks I heard nothing. The hospital switchboard told me that she'd been discharged. I would hurry back from just-show appearances at the laboratory to remain in the apartment and await her call which was never to come. Then finally I received a call from a woman who claimed to be Karin's friend, who knew of my interest in her "welfare" and wanted me first to know that Karin was in Europe (the cries of a baby could be heard in the background and lent veracity to her words) and then she offered me her personal opinion, "if I didn't mind"—and I didn't—that she thought Brian to be a good husband and provider to Karin and that I was encouraging the destruction of their marriage and should weigh also the consequences that would be felt by Molly, Karin's child. I asked where Karin was so I could call her and speak with her directly. She didn't know, she said. What was her address then? She would get it to me, but first would I give her my own so that she could mail it to me? The baby began to cry furiously now and she said she would have to call back. I waited two hours. She never did.

V

Two or three weeks later, I don't remember, I finally reached her at home.

"Hello, Karin."

"Who is this?" she answered, with a coldness I had never heard before. And a shock ripped through me that made me reel.

"It's me, Michael," I said, trying to gloss over the fact that she hadn't recognized my voice.

"I don't know any Michael."

And then I burst, like a paper bag bursts. All that had held me together, made what our year was, the rivets, flowed nonstop out of my mouth—I told her everything, paying meticulous attention to detail. I recounted stories, named restaurants, my apartment, other places we met, told her about a keepsake ring a dying patient had given her, a crèche. I spoke without stopping for nearly half an hour. I recognized that I was finally losing her —but not to the devil that consumes flesh—and in losing

107

her I lost the entire year of meaning of my life. I fought like a drowning man fights. I flailed helplessly, but there was no life preserver thrown me, when finally she responded.

"That ring, I remember, I was sick and another patient, a young girl who was dying, gave me that ring. I can't find it now. How did you know this? Who are you? I can't think, my head hurts so much. But you seem to know a lot about me, how would you know all this if you didn't know me? I am afraid."

"It's all right," I insisted, "it doesn't matter, you'll get your memory back," and I watched my life with her, my only connection, recede like unplugged water in a sink wend its way slowly down the drain. I mustered what little faith in things I had left and asked her if she wanted me to call back, asked her if she could bear it.

"Somehow I'm so afraid," she answered. "I don't know why, but my body is shaking. You know so much. You must know me. But I'm afraid. My mother-in-law said I was in danger; they had to take me away. My head hurts so much."

"Shall I call again," I asked, instilling as much optimism into my voice as I could. "Yes, call; I don't care, call."

I thought it had been electro-shock. That she had been taken by her husband and his "doctors" to a custodial institution in Connecticut that specialized in electrical lobotomies. It had a rich clientele no doubt, and catered especially to the wishes of "loved ones" rather than the patient herself. The wishes were clear in Karin's case.

She had lost perspective again and was deeply depressed. She had declared willingness to commit suicide and had in the not-too-distant past nearly accomplished that. She must not be driven to such passion again, her husband lamented, pointing to her cancer, his career, their family. And the doctors obliged, the disorder in her life would be reduced if not removed entirely.

The skin surface was first scrubbed with alcohol and then coated with electrode paste. The electrodes were flat discs of Monel metal, two-inches in diameter, and applied bilaterally to the skin surface immediate to the medial temporal structures. Employing the technique of Doty, stimulation for ten seconds *produced a retrograde amnesia for the events of the previous three weeks. Twenty sessions would be adequate. While adjunctive hypnotherapy would make the outcome certain. A rubber teething ring was inserted into her mouth to prevent her from biting off her tongue and she was strapped onto the treatment table so as not to break her back, her arms twisted contralaterally in a heavy canvas jacket. The current was generated and sped across her hemispheres, lifting her off the table, removing with each jolt, each convulsion, three weeks of the calendar, three weeks of a life previously lived, obliterating with equality all that was trivial with all that was important, like pages of a book held in contempt they were torn out and thrown away, until the treatment table was pooled*

with urine that washed over onto the floor and
stained the expensive shoes of the psychiatrists and
the white oxfords of the nurses, and soaked to death
the paper slippers that she herself had worn in.

Like a pinball I rebounded off the walls of my apartment. Who was I now that I no longer had her? I was
in a frenzy. I trembled. I picked up the phone and began
to dial some of my co-workers but hung up after the first
few digits. How could I tell people I hardly knew about
the problems of my life. Progress reports were all I
wanted from them. How could I now ask for personal
advice? I picked up the receiver and hung up again—up
and down, several times. Finally I got through to the
Institute psychiatrist. He would see me that afternoon
at the hospital.

I was a stranger now at the Institute, but my research
and my name weren't, people looked at me as though I
were a ghost. I was glad to be back in the hospital halls.
They were comforting now, not demanding. I would
settle with the psychiatrist in a determined, scientific
way what had gone wrong with Karin. Whether I was
to blame. What could be done. The smell of iodoform in
the corridors filled my nostrils, instilled some peace in
me. Disease was being laid away here. Order was being
made. How much did I need this order now!

It was close in Masterson's office. A desk and chair, a
file cabinet on top of which some books were piled and
another chair on which I sat, my head pressed into my
hands for support, was all that could fit. I wondered out

loud whether my thoughts would leave us room to breathe.

I knew he counseled cancer patients as they approached death. What a pittance my needs were compared with theirs. We began in a very professional manner that placed me in the position of colleague making a consultation rather than a supplicant needing consolation, discussing the possibility of different etiologies contributing to her loss of memory. Whether it could have been post-traumatic syndrome following her head injury, or a metastatic throwaway to her brain, or perhaps how she had a schizophrenic episode and sought to remedy things with a conversion reaction, an hysterical forgetting. Then of course the possibility of shock was discussed. "My whole year with Karin was erased parenthetically around me. How could anything but electro-shock accomplish that? Or maybe I was to blame," I offered, as if Masterson was my confessor and could grant me absolution instead of advice. "Was I the wedge that split her? Did I force her into hysteria by not giving her enough honesty and support with which to make a decision? I threatened to separate her from her child. I demanded that she love me, *love* me. I sucked her dry even though I knew she could give no more. Tell me, did I do this to her?" Finally, I let Masterson interrupt.

"I know the pain you're feeling, but don't put yourself to blame. You knew who she was, you would've known if she was schizophrenic. The pervasiveness of her amnesia, covering such a large period of time, would seem to indicate shock rather than psychosis, but it's hard to tell. Try not to worry, give her time. The amnesia will lose its grip."

I ate his words up. I made him repeat them. Made him go through a differential diagnosis of post-traumatic syndrome, conversion reaction, and retrograde amnesia by electro-shock as if we were students again cramming for an exam. Was he sure that I wasn't to blame? "Are you sure I didn't precipitate it?" I demanded again and again. He thought I was taking on too much of the burden. Other forces were at work, forces beyond my control. I should try to take it easy, try to relax. He knew of my problems at the Institute with the skin, he saw a connection, I wasn't guilty as far as he could see, and, moreover, there was no crime.

"Can I call her, do you think? Would it do any more damage?"

"Go easy," he said.

Go easy.

vi

The next day I went back to my lab at the Institute. My associates greeted me with what seemed like an unusually gentle manner. Studiously, I poured over the findings of the last several months. There was nothing but failure. Our own attempts at replication on basic models had failed. The grafts were sloughing off, being rejected by the recipient. Refrigeration no longer mediated a change. What had seemed no longer to matter cast me into deep despair. I was without any ties now. Had no connection. Diplomatically, my juniors had written a note reminding me about the Summer Advisory Meeting with Volner and the Board that was barely two months away and left it on my desk. They too no longer could face me. I don't know for how long I sat there, in a trance—but with a swelling of excitement I considered calling Karin. I suppressed the knowledge of what painful effect my intrusion could have. I wrestled against calling, and I lost. I picked up the receiver with so much

fear, as if I were going to commit an irrevocable act—
but I knew then that I couldn't stop myself. My body
was shaking.

"Karin. . . ."

"Ja . . .," she whispered softly, so softly.

"I called to find out. . . . Listen, forgive me for calling.
I just needed to know if you remembered anything, if
you know who I am. Am I bothering you, please tell
me."

"No," she answered, so softly that the words could
have been generated by no real person. "I'm glad you
called. But, I'm scared. Something in my head hurts me
when I think of you, of what you said. Like a headache,
except it splits down my skull. I found some things you
mentioned. They were downstairs in the storage room.
In a box. I found the ring and a crèche. Did you give me
that?"

"Yes, for Christmas, you were sick."

"And I found the Kotzwinkle book, the Horse Bador-
ties one, and I remembered the story. I heard your voice
reading it to me. Did you do that?"

So weak her voice, so transient, as if she could blow
away. I began to tell her how it was between us. How
much I loved her, how much I needed her now.

"Please," she said, "no more. I cannot listen anymore.
Please."

The phone clicked. I pressed the receiver to my ear.
There were no more words.

A week later I found her letter in my mailbox. I took
it upstairs to my apartment and nervously opened the

envelope. The letter was divided by two dates. It was signed on the bottom by a name she had never used with me before. Almut. The name that was reserved for her family. For her husband.

Dear Michael,

Each time I try to put my thoughts into words, when I try to put them to paper they flee from me—faster and faster from my hands which are not able to grasp them properly. My thoughts do not want to be registered, do not want to be lined up so that you can look at them easily. No! My thoughts are artistic jumps, neat pirouettes, jumping summer-saults, and when they finally flee from me, look back at me, grinning maliciously, playing hide and seek before they finally dissolve into a fine white fog similar to that which rises in the fall from the moist, warm grass, putting the sun behind a veil of mist, giving an inkling of the coming winter. Your face is close to me, a face that demands to be recognized, proud yet humble, the head slightly bent in order to catch still another word, a word which, however, does not want to come over my lips. What you want I cannot give. It lies hidden somewhere under moist, dark green moss, covered by heavy, muddy earth which buries everything—making impossible any breath—it lies on my soul.

Yesterday, I put down the telephone, could not hear any-more your soft but intense voice which whispers into my ear at night, which does not let me sleep. In the park there is no quiet anymore, the trees whisper "Michael, Michael," cars screech "Michael, Michael," each noise seems to call your name, even the noise of jello, and when I close my ears my heart beats in time, "Michael, Michael," and still I cannot get to you—your face before me—I want to touch it—to caress, but my arm is paralyzed, lying at my side heavily as if not belonging to me anymore. Tell me, who holds the strings, who directs my life with such a cool hand? Is it myself at the end? Who tangles the strings until the puppet falls down? My thoughts are enmeshed in this. The waves crash against hard rock, splashing with fury and still not doing anything. They wash across the smooth rock, powerless with their energy, splashing up high but without effect. The rock does not want to recede. The soil behind it is getting dry, remains barren, becomes a desert. Give me time. Let me have more distance from all this. Please don't try to conquer the fortress. It is already besieged and is becoming slowly brittle. Another on-slaught and it will crumble, disintegrate into its elements. Wait until the door opens or better still forget that it ever existed. You can no longer grasp the past. It escaped you. It is too high for your outstretched arms. I jumped higher and higher for only a glimpse—I should recognize it—but my head hurts from the many blows it received. My physical powers are like tired fighters, they lie on the battlefield, lick their wounds and ask for no more and no less than peace. Ask for a cave just large enough to crawl into and close the eyes. I am tired, so tired.

All love,
Almut

vii

I left Brooklyn and drove fifty miles away to Sunken
Meadow Park on Long Island. It was long after rush
hour and there was little traffic on the Southern State
Parkway. Karin went in and out of my mind. The nearly
empty highway had a great calming effect on me. It led
somewhere, if I stayed on it I would arrive at least there.
Defining my position with Karin was impossible for me.
I realized now that I was treading on eggshells in con-
tinuing to call her and that I was eviscerating myself as
well. I knew, felt deep inside of me, that I loved her, that
I had never felt closer to another human being. Yet I had
forced a confrontation that she couldn't deal with alone
and I had given her no support. I had not gone beyond
fantasizing about what I was going to do, never gone up
to Connecticut and taken her away. Why had I held
back? Was I such a coward? I wanted so much for us,
yet couldn't act. And now I fully realized that my impo-
tent demands had accomplished what even the cancer

117

couldn't do, that I had caused her to split in two.

All she asked for now was peace, for a close. I felt sure that her life was on the line, yet I couldn't leave her alone. I resolved not to ask her for anything. I would wait, resist the now terrifying desire to reach out to her. But I would never forget or let the door slam shut. I reached the entrance to the park at 11 p.m., the gate was closed. Angrily, I turned the car around in front of the gate house and headed back to the city.

For three weeks I resisted calling her and then I succumbed. She spoke like a child in short halting sentences. She spoke as if she were far away. I was afraid to say too much, but did anyhow. She could not see me as her husband had enlisted the doorman's help in not allowing her out of the house. But she dreamt of me, an imaginary me, she said, and wanted to see my face, see if it matched. "I must hang up now," her voice almost whistled, low and secretive.

⋮⋮⋮
viii

I don't remember how long it was after that she agreed to meet me at the county park in Westchester where we had met a long time ago. It was early July and the sun was out. It was a perfect day for remembrances, except I wasn't sure that the past was going to be remembered or even that I would be recognized. I examined my face carefully in the rear-view mirror of my car, pulling my face in and out until I presented what I felt was me, and headed out of the city fearful that Karin wasn't going to recognize me at all. To make matters worse I forgot the way. I passed the park and had to retrack an additional five miles in heavy traffic. She told me that she had only three hours free and the first half-hour was already gone. I was sure she would think I hadn't come. Recklessly I went through red lights and finally reached the park. It took another half an hour to find her.

She was sitting on a blanket with what I took to be her daughter not too far from the place we once sat huddled together in a union we thought unbreakable. Before I approached her, I looked at her from across the pond. She was the same beautiful woman. She hadn't changed. Her daughter sat on a tricycle and rode around the blanket. Karin stared at the pond. She hardly moved. I was afraid to move, but convinced myself that she would recognize me. I walked toward her. No smile came across her face as she met my eyes. No greeting. I kneeled on one knee before her.

"Hello, Karin, do you remember me?" I forced a smile.

She studied my face carefully and after a while spoke. Her daughter ignored us, riding round and round the blanket. "I thought you would be blond and tall. I mean from your voice on the phone. I didn't see you like this."

I almost apologized for looking as I did, but swallowed it, putting, as they say, my best face forward. "How are you?" I gently enquired, keeping all my emotion in check.

"I'm all right," she said, then introduced me to Molly, who ignored us and pedalled away.

I took out a pack of cigarettes and offered her one. They were Gitanes. She accepted and held up the cigarette.

"Short and fat, just like Frenchmen," and for the first time her face broke into a broad grin.

I turned on my stomach and she followed, we looked at the path above the grassy slope, our backs to the pond. I began to question her and provide answers for questions she hadn't posed; I attempted to sew together a blanket of remembrance, but I soon saw it would be impossible. I didn't press anymore. We talked of little things. So much. I can hardly remember. I just remember her face, her eyes, and the eyelashes she once asked if I minded. I wanted to take her into my arms and cry, but there wasn't any way for that. There was glass between us—we could see one another, speak through the small holes, but couldn't touch. Molly came over and asked to go to the see-saw across the park. We folded the blanket and followed Molly across the grass. Karin remarked how incredible it was that the three of us, who had never really met before—though of course she believed my story, she added—appeared so much like a family. So much so that the people on the benches who watched our procession wouldn't have believed otherwise.

Molly and I mounted the see-saw, Karin holding the child at her end. We went up and down several times until Molly demanded to be let down. Once down she picked up a stone and threw it at me. "Don't you touch my Mommy," she cried. I promised her that I wouldn't.

There was no settlement of course, we drove in our separate cars to an ice-cream stand on the highway. While on line to get Molly a cone, a young woman approached Karin and asked how she was. It was apparent that Karin didn't recognize her. The woman advertised sex all over her. "What a fucked-up place. I left soon after you," she told the completely uncomprehending Karin, who stared at her as at an apparition. "People do this," she told me, "they come over to me as if they know me from some place before. Maybe they do know me. Maybe I just forgot."

I bought Molly her ice-cream cone.

A week later a small parcel from Karin arrived in the mail. There was a small bound notebook inside. The pages of the notebook were blank except for the first several, on which Karin had written *Ein Märchen!* a fairy tale. On the first page was the penciled drawing of a bird in flight.

Once upon a time there was a King who somehow managed to peacefully govern his little kingdom. He owned three treasures. A treasure house which he entered every morning and every evening, very suspiciously, to count his riches. He also owned a rosebush so lovely and fragrant that anybody who saw it was entirely embraced by its prettiness. And thirdly, he owned a Princess who was not really pretty, not wise, but she belonged to him. The King and his subjects had only one wish and one desire, and this was to organize their kingdom as perfectly as possible. Even the smallest details were organized according to a detailed plan and even the life inside was completely brought into harmony with the outside. So it is no wonder that no soul at any time put its foot outside the kingdom. Yes, if somebody would have mentioned such an idea, the subjects of the King would most likely declare him insane since each little child knew that outside the kingdom there was only disorder and chaos and this did not agree with the sense of harmony and prettiness of these people. Well, only the Princess sometimes looked into the distance with a desirous look, sighed a little bit and yearned for things which were not entirely perfect in form, their colors not harmonizing with everything else. The main occupation of the Princess was to care for the rosebush which she had raised from a seed. It is entirely the truth that there was no prettier rosebush in the whole kingdom. The Princess spent many hours in order to fertilize and water and cut the twigs of the rosebush so that the bush took on the right form. But, more often, she was struck by an inexplicable restlessness and finally one day, neglecting all interdictions, she climbed over the wall which was built around the little kingdom to protect it and she saw how nice and wonderful it smelled outside. The air was filled with the singing of birds and full of fragrances. There were many colorful panoramas before her eyes. Oh, how wonderful it smelled. The air was full of songs and fragrances. A colorful panorama lay before her eyes which she could not have dreamt about ever. The Princess walked a few steps, became more and more adventuresome, and went further and further away from her castle. She was entirely overpowered from all the prettiness and finally she sat down on a tree trunk and fell into a deep sleep. She was awakened by a marvelous melody which came from a pretty bird which had sat down on her lap. She enticed him to one song after the other until she felt that her heart would break with joy and sorrow. From this day on, the Princess left the castle more and more often and the pretty bird led her to the highest mountains and into the darkest canyons and taught her on a misty, foggy day to see the sunshine and that a seemingly dead world could awake to bustling busyness. Now the absence of the Princess came to the ears of the King and he thought how he could keep her. He soon realized that he could not do anything to the bird because he could never catch him and the Princess would probably not voluntarily give up the bird. At that point, he remembered the old witch who lived somewhere in the dark forest and he immediately went to her to ask her to help him. The King crossed through marshy moors and dark and whispering forests until he finally and tirefully knocked at her door. "Come in, come in Söhnchen," said the old witch. "I know why you have come to me, but it will cost you something, ja, ja, ja." With these words, she extended her claws after the purse of the King and for a short moment her eyes glistened with great desire for the gold. "Well, here," said the witch, "take this flask, it will give you what you want and even something more. Just put it in her wine." And with these words she shoved the frightened King out of her door. He hastened back home immediately and did as she told him. The Princess drank the cup until the last drop and immediately fell into a deep, deep sleep. In the meantime, the bird was waiting for his playmate, and when she didn't arrive he flew into her castle window straight into her bedroom, sat down on her bed and started to sing. Soon she opened her eyes and asked, "Where does this strange bird come from? Chase him away, he is interrupting my sleep." Astounded, the bird looked at the girl but her eyes showed him his own reflection as if it were in a mirror. As much as he sang, he could not make one bit of remembrance or movement in the Princess. At that point, he flew up sorrowfully and quietly away. The Princess again cared the entire day for the rosebush and only the rosebush could warm up the frozen heart of the Princess a little bit. The King again reigned, the bird sang his pretty songs and bewitched each being in the forest with his sorrowful melodies, and if they did not die then they still live on today!

Das Ende.

That evening I received a call from the Director's personal secretary. The Summer Advisory Meeting had convened and I was to make my presentation the next morning at nine. Volner had arrived from England. He would be there. I decided to go to the Institute that night and sleep in my office. I couldn't bear staying in the apartment anymore.

I threw my bag onto my desk and took the elevator to the top floor. From there I climbed to the roof. It was a warm night and most of Manhattan lay visible before me. I thought nothing about skin or of the meeting the next day. I looked at the hospital next door, at the lighted windows, at the tiny cubicles and the lives inside. Occasionally I spotted a television screen. A nurse entering a room. Or the white gown of a patient. The dying no longer concerned me, I was no longer afraid. The lights shimmering in the distance caused me to lose my focus as they moved in and out of place. Twenty stories below lay the narrow street, deserted except for a few cars that looked like ants. I thought of the Director's cat who had plunged to his death the year before from the penthouse next door. I thought of Karin and how I had become her assassin. Nothing made sense anymore. Why had it happened like this? To the south the Queensboro Bridge stretched across the East River, the spans lit up like a diamond necklace on a black woman's breast. We could have shared it together. Suddenly I became terribly nauseated and sank to my knees. Shock waves erupted from my stomach and I spewed my bile off the roof of the Institute. Noiselessly it reached the pavement below. When the vomitus was exhausted, I continued to heave. I wanted to spill my guts.

I set the lab clock and fell asleep in my clothes on a couch in the outer office. I awoke before the alarm to the bitter taste in my mouth and after gargling sought to wash my shirt which was heavily stained. At eight, I took the elevator to the twentieth floor where the laboratory animals were kept. The five adjoining rooms were filled with hundreds of barking, screaming dogs and a stench of urine so strong that a gauze mask is worn by the attendants who work there. The dogs were caged in rows of two-level tiers, cages that for the larger dogs were too narrow to allow them to lie down and too shallow to permit them to stand. The cages were metal and were closed on all but one side. On the door of each cage was a piece of adhesive tape with the dog's weight in kilograms and, in the case of an already-chosen dog, the experimenter's name with special instructions as to care and feeding. Urine and fecal matter dripped from the upper cages to the lower. The accumulated waste was being decimated by high-pressure hoses wielded without regard for the dogs by the green-uniformed attendants in rubber hip-boots. My shoes were submerged in the inch of water that filled the room.

In an upper cage by the wall just in front of the door, a dog was being considered by two attendants. He was a "good donor dog," the one said, his weight was good and he was apparently healthy. The donor dog is sacrificed in order to provide the blood for another dog that will undergo experimental surgery. "Those operated dogs can never get enough blood," the other attendant said to me. I couldn't pass them easily now, so I stood and watched.

The attendant nearest me opened the cage door swiftly and in a moment his companion had adhesive-taped the startled dog's mouth shut. A stick with a lasso at the end was passed around his neck and tightened. The dog began to retreat in fear to the back wall of the cage and with a sharp yank was pulled with a thud six feet to the water-covered floor. The dogs in the room began howling again. Shivering now in terror, his legs were tightly bound with cord and tape. One attendant grabbed a paw and used an electric clipper to shave the skin and expose an underlying vein. He was then injected with an anesthetic and the syringe unscrewed from the needle. In its place a heparinized blood-Pak container was connected. While I watched, pint after pint of blood was emptied from his body. I couldn't move. I stood transfixed. Incontinent, his coat was stained with defecation, his eyes appeared to explode. The last pint required the attendant to forcefully massage the chest with his boot in order to drain as much of the remainder as possible. The dying dog's blood would help keep his mate alive.

Numb, I stepped over the shuddering donor dog and walked through the last room to the door that led to the hospital. Two flights down was the experimental wing and my old subject Anthony Lukash. His forehead had been completely reclaimed by white skin. It was impossible to tell there had ever been a graft. He registered surprise at seeing me again, and I told him that some people from England would be examining him soon and that they wanted to inspect the area that lost the graft. I said I was going to inject a chemical into his skin that would make the area more visible to them. I filled a 2cc syringe with a black dye used for tumography. Within minutes, the dye began to invest the tissue, inch by inch, until it appeared that Lukash was wearing a skullcap which covered his forehead at a rakish angle. Now they wouldn't be disappointed.